WRITTEN ON A BODY

Severo Sarduy

WRITTEN ON A BODY

Translated by Carol Maier

Lumen Books

Lumen Books
446 West 20 Street
New York, NY 10011

Printed in the United States of America
ISBN: 0-930829-04-2

Originally published as *Escrito sobre un Cuerpo*

Lumen Books are produced by Lumen, Inc., a tax-exempt, non-profit organization. This publication was made possible, in part, with public funds from the New York State Council on the Arts and the National Endowment for the Arts.

Contents

Translator's Introduction

By gathering them into a single energy—the drive of simulation—*Written on a Body* connects dissimilar phenomena taken from heterogenous and apparently unconnected spaces, which range from the organic to the imaginary, from the biological to the baroque: animal mimesis (defensive?), tattooing, human transvestism (sexual?), make-up, mimickry dress art, anamorphosis, trompe-l'oeil.

The space where this galaxy expands is that of Painting and Literature: reflection and homage.

Severo Sarduy, *La simulación*[1]

The suggestion that simulation is an essential, biological force promises an exhilarating freedom for a translator, that most mimetic of readers who is ever aware how much her work will inevitably be something of a disappointment, a mere attempt at likeness, a flawed reproduction. By apparently legitimizing, even welcoming transgression, Severo Sarduy's definition seems to contend that the original is the *copy,* that the simulacrum throbs with life. Or, to follow a step further, the figures "making their rounds" in the opening paragraph of *Written on a Body*—and such a step must be taken for the full importance of that initial alternation to be evident—it is as if what is commonly considered the original called for its own death, as if, breast bared, it placed a knife in the reader's hand, all the while speaking encouragement and reassurance about simulation as a natural, life-engendering phenomenon. That same original even presents a strategy, a highly ludic and dynamic approach to forming a simulacrum from a subtle blend of admiration and laughter tinged with derision (the reflection that accompanies Sarduy's homage may well ponder or reconsider more than it mirrors). New vitality is thus guaranteed as life is taken. What is more—and, although this is only alluded to in the introductory definition, it becomes explicit in the essays—, Sarduy's "original" is itself a complex simulacrum "in action." As such, it simultaneously constructs and shatters an intricate, often highly oblique representation of Hispanic, or, more specifically, Cuban reality.

Those last two sentences may seem to contradict somewhat Sarduy's clear affirmation of simulation by introducing a potentially far-reaching ambiguity, but the contradiction is essential and appropriate to the primary gesture or motion within the essays. As if to echo a reminder by José Lezama Lima that because it challenges, only "resistance . . . is able to ruffle, arouse, and sustain our capacity for knowledge,"[2] the motion that directs *Written on a Body* is as much one of defiance as reception. Far from acquiescing in their own demise, Sarduy's words make heavy demands on the reader and present a would-be simulator with some challenging passages. Nor is the breast they offer truly bared since the skin writhes with apparently indecipherable hieroglyphics. The sentences are long and convoluted, and Sarduy's use of other writers and their work is as elusive as it is constant. Even when a reader is acquainted with the many French and Hispanic sources, Sarduy's *bricolage* ("Free Texts and Plane Texts") entangles as well as tantalizes. An invitation to create a reading, a simulacrum, is extended, but clearly for Sarduy a "good" original makes reading an arduous and tricky process in which his reader is forced to experience an intense, aggressive exchange of energy. Goaded on by desire to understand, but frustrated by complexity and annoyed by a suspicion that the final outcome of so much effort may be an assemblage of words ripped from their contexts, made to say something other than—even the reverse of—what they mean, the reader cries out for help, mercy, or divine intervention.

That such an abrasively ludic poetics will directly influence its own translation should be immediately evident. I would like, nevertheless, to comment on two convergent but closely related ways in which I was aware of the poetics of *Written on a Body* as I prepared the present translation. In the first place, Sarduy's celebration of simulation has encouraged me to accept and even enjoy the play of translation (not only as pleasure but also as drama, a staged representation that occurs in a carefully defined area). I have therefore been able to shed, or at least set aside, much of my inclination—one articulated by many translators—to lament the dependent nature of my work and apologize for inescapable gaps between my version and the Spanish original. With respect to language, syntax in particular, this has meant that on occasion I felt free to reorder or even divide a long sentence incapable of breathing in English, no matter how it was punctuated, or when I was certain there were cries from the English-speaking reader coming not from breakthrough but exasperation somewhere beyond the point of endurance. By the same token, in several other instances I have combined very short paragraphs in deference to the English reader's unfamiliarity with the Spanish propensity for developing ideas in long sentences but short paragraphs. On still other occasions, and without feeling compelled to add a note of explanation, I have departed from a literal translation in favor of a more spontaneous solution in English. For example, I have found it not only justifiable but also imperative to construct my own *bricolage* when a "faithful" translation would have failed to let a careful reader make necessary connections between Sarduy's essays, his other work (both in Spanish and in English translation), and the work of other writers.

This principle of *bricolage* and Sarduy's continuous appropriation and adaptation has also guided my translation of his "quotations" and my use of material by other translators. Although I did consult his sources in the original, I have translated those sources as they appear (or in some cases *dis*appear) in the essays, even when I saw that a quotation was incomplete or that it had been deformed slightly in order for it to conform to a new context. When the works Sarduy used are available in English translation, I have indicated that in the notes. I have also consulted those translations and in many instances woven them directly into my text. In other cases, however, I either have not used the English version or have deformed it slightly so it would conform to its new context. None of the alterations is explained, but my tracks are there to be followed and questioned. I am fully aware of the "unprofessional" nature of this lack of complete documentation, especially when using expertly translated work by highly competent translators. At the same time, the more I studied Sarduy's essays with an eye to his sources, the more certain I became of the need to translate the act of simulation as well as the words used to describe it. This meant working in an analogous way with *my* sources to create a deliberately unscholarly text where the notes at the foot of the page are wisps, loose ends that suggest unraveling rather than buttressing.

Which brings me, albeit indirectly, to the second way that Sarduy's text influenced my translation. Or perhaps I should say "paradoxically" rather than "indirectly," for that second influence has to do with a fidelity quite different from, even the inverse of, the affirmation of difference I have just described. Here I refer to my conviction that a considerable amount of foreignness and uncertainty is necessary if the English-speaking reader is to approximate the reading experience in Spanish. Since resistance is an integral part of the simulation Sarduy presents as a complex natural process, it would be a disservice to both languages if his writing were made more accessible, if the reader were eased toward what might—mistakenly—be called comprehension by shortening many of the long sentences, smoothing them out. Equally unjust would be an expectation or a hope that the creation of a successful simulacrum in English might provide a reading in which the translated condition of a work would be imperceptible. A distinct sense of discomfort is crucial to *Written on a Body*; in fact it marks, so to speak, the accurate translation of an estrangement felt by many readers in Spanish to whom Sarduy also sounds foreign and translated, although from a somewhat different perspective. (This perspective, I might add, cannot but be "lost" in translation, since it is impossible to convey to an English-speaking reader at a different moment in history the impact on a Latin American reader of the Parisian Spanish in *Escrito sobre un cuerpo*[3] or of the "gaudy transvestites" from *La simulación*).

The reader's acknowledged experience of the marginal, then, is the translator's principal objective, and what I have endeavored to create in English is a place of dense superimposition that is also a motion, a turning on (as in both "over" and "against") self to turn into the endless flip of edges, the periodic outbursts that constitute Cuban reality as conveyed in Sarduy's verbal constructs. My own greatest bind no doubt occurred as I realized that the success of my efforts would depend on the striking of a precarious, impossibly perfect imbalance between analogy and separation. I was aware, for example, that just as Zukofsky's "travesty" of Catullus may be the "*bridge* that links his world to our own,"[4] so might a similarly extravagant translation of Sarduy be the one that would best capture the extreme ellipsis, the anamorphosis, the distance intensified to intimacy that determine his representation of Cuba. I also realized, however, that my translation would not be the most recent in a series made throughout centuries, but the first; and I realized that my author is not a "classic" but a writer unfamiliar to English-speaking readers, one who does not quite fit with what they have come to consider the "mainstream" of Latin American literature.

For those reasons, although a concession to likeness, to a considerable resemblance between original and simulacrum, means that there might be readers who wished for a translation that stretched

Sarduy's work further by placing his situations as well as his words in English, it seemed better to err on the side of a readily perceptible likeness. This meant, for example, retaining not only Lezama Lima but also the referents and the Cubanness of the original rather than trying to leap to a version that might have proved more Sarduyan, but only if it were able to resonate, like Zukofsky's Catullus, in a spectrum of other translations. In the absence of that spectrum, I preferred to distort English, to Cubanize it, in a way that seemed most appropriate for the present. It is my hope that, along with Sarduy's fiction and his plays[5], the essays in *Written on a Body* will introduce a bit of *choteo*[6] and thereby contribute to the provocation of a less uniform, more dynamic reading of Latin American literature in English.

I am grateful to Severo Sarduy for his kind answers to my many questions and for the friendship he extended to me throughout the long process of translation. If doubts remain, it is because I failed to ask the right questions or to utilize his responses fully. I am also grateful for Sarduy's request that *Written on a Body* include not only the essays comprised in *Escrito sobre un cuerpo* but also a long section from *La simulación*. Although I was not fully aware of it when I began, as my work progressed, I came to realize that by combining essays written over a period of fifteen years, Sarduy had created what is in effect a new book whose chapters can be read as pieces of a single poetics.

I also want to thank Ronald Christ for his invitation to translate *Escrito sobre un cuerpo*, for his invaluable questions and suggestions, for his patience; Octavio Armand for a careful reading of the entire manuscript in both languages, for his constant collaboration and his generosity; Maryanne Bertram, George Chambers, and Fred Maier for their readings (and their rereadings) of individual sections; Marina Savoie and her colleagues at the Bradley University Library for enabling me to carry out my research; the many friends, in particular Eugene Sigel, who answered questions related to this project.

Carol Maier
Kent, 24 August 1989

Copy / Simulacrum

Wicker hampers piled at the far end of a white patio, very white light. From the garden pond with its dozing Chinese fish, to the hampers, a passageway between brick walls, a second, humid patio of Areca palms; the thick whitewash on the walls is shaded by huge red mobile studs of flamboyant. There is no murmur of doves.

From the pond to the street, in the opposite direction from the scene above, the dining room opens on the patio of propped shadows, adorned with a plain, somewhat ochre still life.

The table always set: Zubaranesque cloth of studied folds, earthenware compote—cashews, soursops, medlars, fleshy red oriental mangoes spotted with yellow and black—, polyhedral pitcher of water—a lamentable Lezamesque because of the possible linear reflection, positioned and purple on the fine-loomed linen: in our family we did not usually drink wine.

At the center, a ceramic lamp, solemn like an insular reference to Gaudí, stylized floral motifs, vegetal whorls, a black frame continually dashed by hummingbirds blinded in the noonday heat.

Colonial or disproportionate rockers, small white flagstones, a large mahogany cupboard full of embroidered fichus, with a bell in the latch.

Outside, the paved, empty street. Silence. A buggy with its handles resting on the ground. There is no wind. Heaviness. Baroque siesta.

Another street, this one dirt. Iron windows, unmatched hinges. We have everything decorated for the celebration of Saint John the Baptist: from front to back, small cellophane flags, flowers on the sidewalk, chickens and pigs: the block has decided to abuse a country theme in our decorations for the Carnival contest; machetes and guano hats summarize the neighbors' hurried Sunday best.

That slut you see at the right, between a parrot on its hoop and a turkey, dressed in tomato red with her high heels sunk in the mud, shaking with a convulsive shriek of laughter that has set swaying atop her head a large tuft of turkey feathers and a diamond tiara—in the photograph, a string of small lights with clear, scribbly points—, that whore with Moorish eyes holding a large fan is none other than yours truly.

It is afternoon and it might have rained. My father and I decide to dress up. He'll go as a scarecrow or a ghost—a mask caked with paint or a sheet—, I put on the flashiest getup I can find in a drawer inherited from my mother. When I step into the street, teetering as if on stilts, my father closes the door and shouts: "There she goes!" He comes out after mc and we're off dancing. We've been drinking Santiago *prú*. Our rumbas and congas unwind through the adjacent blocks, which, without dissimulation, are Venetian—beached gondolas—, Galician, Chinese—one of my cousins, whose father is Chinese, receives the bedecked notables in a kimono, her two coils of hair pierced by rhinestone-studded pins; seated on the floor of a transparent pagoda made of bamboo and sheets of cellophane, she is demure and appropriately enigmatic: we are offered tea.

I'm laughing now like a queen, rather I'm convulsed with pyloric spasms: because instead of broody hens, boughs of *guásima*, goats and rabbits, I see myself on a splendid set, very low black lacquered furniture with straight angles, tapestries with white circles, columns of fragmented mirrors. On the dark tables, golden branches in slender Japanese vases; Turkish screens and cushions, mauve and silver, opaque lamps: on metal, irridescent crystal disks. Wide stairways with curved, highly varnished bannisters punctuated by naked, torch-bearing caryatids. The waltz begins.

I'm laughing, then, at everything, but harder now, because I'm laughing at people who laugh—at me—, at laughter itself, at the tiny mocking death that appears to me from behind the Viennese screens, its white eyelids sewn shut.

Am I simulating? What? Whom? My mother, a woman, my father's wife? Woman? Or rather: the ideal woman, the essence, which is to say, the model and the copy have struck up a relationship of impossible correspondence and nothing is conceivable as long as there is an effort to make one of the terms *be* an image of the other: *to make what is the same be what it is not*. In order for everything to signify it is necessary to accept that I am not inhabited by duality but by an *intensity of simulation* that constitutes its own end, outside of whatever it imitates: what is simulated? Simulation.

And now, surrounded by curtains and cushions reminiscent of Rubén Darío, with a background of screens and waltzes—amidst large birds and chickens—only I reign here, traversed by simulation, magnetized by the reverberation of an appearance, emptied by convulsions of laughter: abolished, absent.

EROTICISMS

FROM *YIN* TO *YANG*

(About Sade, Bataille, Marmori, Cortázar, and Elizondo)

To Octavio Paz and Marie José

Everything leads us to believe in the existence of a certain spiritual point at which we stop perceiving life and death, the real and the imaginary, the past and the future, the communicable and the incommunicable as contradictory.

André Breton, *Second Manifesto*

SADE

Fixity

The *Dance of Life and Death*, with its rhythm of candied hats, gestures hindered by jewels, flowers and fruits, and of frozen monarchs, its periodic rounds of brocades and bleeding skeletons, arabesques and skulls, is inscribed, decipherable, on the more discursive than erotic, more thoughtful than licentious, pages of the Marquis de Sade.

A scansion of *vanities* and corruptions, Life Is Passing. That medieval certainty, which gave rise to macabre dances on Romanesque frescoes and corollas of frenetic skulls on Gothic miniatures and tympanums, that Christian conviction, translated into the materialistic vocabulary of the age and lacking the mirage of a possible redemption (crude tombs tumbling open for the Resurrection and the explosion of bugles that lend their golden celebration to the pages of an evangelistary) is inscribed in the Marquis's exemplary texts: "In all living things, the beginning of life is nothing but death itself; we receive and nourish them both within ourselves at the same time. . . . Matter, deprived of the other subtle portion of matter that transmitted motion, is not destroyed: it changes form, rots, and in so doing offers proof of motion that preserves: it nourishes, fertilizes the earth, contributes to the regeneration of other kingdoms, as well as to its own."[1] Sade's thought feeds on that becoming, that unceasing reconversion, that cycle in which growth and decline are like the facets of a Möbius strip: they occur without a break, without requiring the path that follows them to cross over from *the other side*, skip a facet, encounter an edge.[2]

In *Sade mon prochain*, Pierre Klossowski has shown how, for Sade, "only motion is real: living creatures represent no more than changing phases." Klossowski has likened this idea to the Indian doctrine of Samsara.

It is easy to understand how the history of sadism, that fascination with motion which the ideology of an eighteenth-century Provençal nobleman turned into a cultural event and inscribed in the realm of the imaginary—which not only differentiates his experience from but also opposes it to those of Gilles de Rais[3] and Erzsébet Báthory[4]—, would be dominated, lacerated, by the phantom of *fixity*. To fix, to prevent motion. Hence, his rhetoric of fastening, of knots, of whatever curtails the Other and thus, because of the law of contrast, restores the sadist's total free will, returns him to the initial state of absolute possibility, liberates him, "unties" him.

Theater

Into sadistic aggression the panoply of the object introduces a *code of the act* (in the theatrical sense of that word as well). Theater as the space of performance, as the demand for a breach—a scene—viewed from without, a spectacle, is present in every one of Sade's works. Thus, in Sade, writing fulfilled its essential mission of *dis-alienation*, since that type of theater, breach and spectacle, was created during twenty years of imprisonment; created, in other words, from solitude and confinement. Prison demanded its opposite: theater; cell: stage. The Marquis was not only an author (from erotic pieces and tragedies, like *Jeanne Laisné*, to moral dramas and tear-jerkers, like *Oxtiern ou les malheurs du libertinage*), an actor (he had played a part in the performance of *Oxtiern* at Versailles in 1799 and, of course, acted in La Coste), and a prompter (at Versailles, during the Revolution), but also a precursor who invented psychodrama when, during his last imprisonment in Charenton, he staged plays with the inmates confined there.

That the object as signifier of the sadistic *act* probably found its best definition in another cell (this time in a convent) proves how constant certain structural relations are. When Fra Angelico painted his *Christ Scorned* on the wall of a cell in the convent of San Marco at Florence, he offered an iconic model of objects (as well as of the hands that make use of them), placing his impressive fetishes at the center of that trilogy whose terms would be confinement, theater, sadism.

In the foreground of the scene are seated the Virgin and a saint who seems to be turning the pages of a book open on his knees, a visible symmetry of gestures, of thin, very white hands. In the background, on a dais, in front of a dark rectangle that, like the flat of a stage set, stands out in relief against the wall behind, a blindfolded Christ in a plain robe endures his humiliation without relinquishing his symbolic scepter or transparent sphere. Superimposed clearly on the panel, a second halo of sadistic emblems surrounds the crowned head of the martyr. On his right, one hand is about to slap his face, while above the head of a young tormentor who spits on him another hand lifts a hat, as if in mock reverence. A third hand points to the victim, clutching between its fingers something that the condition of the fresco (or of my memory and of the reproductions I have consulted) makes it impossible to discern. On the martyr's left, one hand threatens him and another brandishes a thin stick that strangely resembles his scepter.

In this way, the emblems of torture emerge from the darkness of the panel: gestures of an obscure sign language, a heraldry of object-acts.

Passion, Repetition

It is not by chance that the Passion provides the first image in the sadistic sequence. Sadism, as an ideology, entails a space that is first *Christian* (which Sade makes the object of his refutation and mockery), then *deist*, and, finally, ruled by an evil God. Because the machinery of belief and the authority of God (or the King, who is his metaphor) have been toppled, the master/slave dialectics can be established. The servant no longer obeys in the name of something (which he reveres in the act of servitude), but only in the name of the law of the strongest.

That refutation of divine imposture takes pleasure in continual reiteration. Not because the atheist's "scientific" truth demands it, but because such rejection, that reverse prayer, that other conjuring, all have erotic value.

An erotic act, blasphemy devotes each *scene* to mocking invisible power (God) in order to permit the fall of visible power (the King); it claims each act in the name of atheism and revolution.

But not only blasphemy is repeated. Repetition (also according to the meaning of the word in French: the *rehearsal* of a work) is the last support of the sadistic imagination and, doubtless, of all perversion.

To become perverted is not only to increase the gestures of sexuality but also to reduce them. If it is true that all the possibilities are exploited in Sade, this is only, as Sade himself explains, so that each reader can discover his pleasure. The pervert explores an instant; in the vast array of sexual combination only a *game* seduces and justifies him. But that instant, fleeting among all others, in which the configuration of his desire materializes, recedes increasingly, moves further and further beyond his reach, as if something falling, something going astray were about to crack, to open a hiatus, a break between reality and desire. Vertigo of that unreachable instant, perversion is the repetition of the gesture confident of reaching it. And in hopes of seizing the unattainable, of joining reality and desire, of coinciding with his own ghost, the pervert breaks every law. In "Kant avec Sade," Jacques Lacan has shown how Sade's hero renounces subjectivity in order to attain his goal. At the center of Sadism, there is no subject; sadism is the object's unadulterated search. The Kantian hero, if one existed, would be exactly the opposite: for him there would be no object to overtake; all that mattered would be a morality devoid of any goal, would be pure subject.

A moral subject without an object, the Kantian hero would be healthy; as the subject-less search, the sadist is a perverse hero. The search of that object, lost forever but forever present in its deception, reduces the sadistic system to repetition. In order to reach fulfillment of desire it is necessary to create optimum conditions. Hence the precise, inflexible code of positions and gestures prescribed by Sade. Each night is a rehearsal of optimum conditions.

Like an actor waiting in the wings for an image, for the utterance of a word, for a light before he steps into the space of the open, the glance, the Other, so Sade's hero waits in the orgy of his nightly rehearsal for the formation of that scene where reality will depict his desire.

But if repetition is the support of all perversion, it is also the support of all ritual. Conjuring, spells, and the succession of *tableaux vivants* that constitute the orgy all demand identical care; they involve a similar memorization of stage directions and precepts, and their desires and purposes are analogous.

The precise code of the invocation, with its requirements of work and gesture, is no more than the prescription of optimum conditions in order that a presence, the divine presence, might appear and validate the participation of objects, might become incarnate and bestow the quality of *being* on what was previously only *thing*. The code of the orgy, with its exact instructions, prescribes optimum conditions in order that something unattainable by definition—the erotic phantom—might coincide with the physical fact of bodies and justify with its presence the display of forces and blasphemy.

Orgy and Mass: rites of equal ambitions, equal futilities.

BATAILLE

The Small Death

"The violence of spasmodic happiness is deep within my heart, deep. And that violence, I tremble to say, is at the same time the center of the death opening within me." This sentence from the prologue to *Les Larmes d'Éros* could define, limit, the sphere in which Georges Bataille's work expresses the identity of opposites, as if the West conceived the existence of a *circle of sensation*. Coincidence of "voluptuousness, delirium, and limitless horror"; similarity "between horror and a voluptuousness that transcends me, between my final pain and an unbearable happiness"; identity of the *small death* (that French metaphor for ejaculation) and final death.[5]

But if eroticism renders the antipodes identical, that is because its true meaning escapes reason, for reason "has never been able to measure its limits''; ''the meaning of eroticism escapes those who do not see a *religious* meaning in it.''

By creating guilt, prohibition, religion forces sexuality to draw back toward the zone of secrecy, toward that zone where prohibition gives the forbidden act an opaque clarity at once ''sinister and divine,'' a murky clarity that belongs to ''obscenity and crime,'' and also to religion.

The iconography of *Les Larmes d'Éros* ranges from bas-reliefs representing the ''open'' sexual act (figures lying on their backs head to toe, toe to head) and visual puns from the Aurignacian Age (a feminine nude that becomes a phallus if the spectator's position changes) to two recent photographic sequences.

The first sequence corresponds to a voodoo ceremony in which the initiate, covered with blood and white feathers, drinks from a goat's head and enters an ''ecstasy similar to drunkenness''; the second sequence corresponds to the Leng Tch'e, a Chinese torture, and was taken by Carpeaux in Peking in 1905. In these latter photographs, which were very important to his work, Bataille discovered a ''great power in inversion'' (*renversement*) after learning about the discipline of Yoga. The last page of *Les Larmes d'Éros* stresses a ''fundamental relation: the relation between religious ecstasy and eroticism, sadism in particular.''

The power of the photograph as evidence, its unbearable ''this has happened,'' its analogical *reality*, constitute the initial *node* or ''kernel'' in several stories by Bataille.

On his deathbed, in that ''terror of infinity renewed by old age,'' as he wrote the book he would leave unfinished, Bataille returned to the source of his fiction, of his life: ''The beginning, which I glimpse at the edge of the grave, is that of the *pig* in me which neither death nor insult can kill. At the edge of the grave terror is divine. I plunge myself into that terror whose son I am.''

In that return to the beginning, which illuminates the proximity of death and Bataille's awareness of it, in the unfinished pages of *Ma mère* (*My Mother*), the first thing we find—an abominable and posthumous opening—is a series of photographs. In them, obscenity and crime mingle to the point of ridiculousness: ''The licentious, obscene photographs of that period resorted to strange procedures whose comic and repugnant elements were aimed at making the photographs more effective, more shocking.'' But in those images there is beauty and love (the idea of ''conversion'' has its source here), since the person who appears in them, in "revolting positions," is the mother of Pierre, the narrator. His mother and shame are now linked forever: God and horror. "God is the horror in me of what was, is, and will be so horrible that at any cost I should refuse and shout with all my strength that I deny it ever happened, happens, or will happen, although if I were to do that I would be lying."

Since, in a single space of yellowish shadows, actual photographs, absolute witnesses, guarantees of what "happened," join forever what Pierre most loves and most hates ("my father and my mother in a swamp of obscenity"), he cannot help but "despair, and follow his horror all the way through to its end." Here, on one of the last pages he wrote, Bataille states most clearly the fusion of antipodes, the inseparable union of love and horror. Georges Bataille is about to die; Pierre, the narrator of his last book, embraces life when he discovers the obscene photographs: "Within me happiness and terror drew tight a suffocating knot. I was suffocating and moaning from pleasure. *The more those images terrified me, the more they aroused me.*"

Motion and Watch

Like a river, like the continuous sentence, the incessant text that begins with our speech and is only ended by death, so thought (which is perhaps nothing but that sentence, and in no way either anticipates or exceeds it) flows, monotonous, rambling, linear, unselfconscious in pure motion. The insertion of the awareness of evil into the flow of this thought-in-motion provokes, with its irradiation of a foreign body, an interruption, a "cut" that turns thought back on itself, as if reflected by a mirror, and reduces it to that questioning of its own existence which, for Bataille, is the essence of philosophy.

No longer the victim of its activity but on the *watch*, this thought has overcome the limits of morality, because it lives Good and Evil, tensely, as an irresistible attraction of antipodes.

When thought awakens, when it suddenly finds itself confronting those objects it had always excluded for reasons of comfort and prejudice, it turns into philosophy; and, as Denis Hollier explains, for Bataille philosophizing is death: "Like eroticism and sacrifice, the awakening of thought makes us live a small death."[6]

Bataille's writing unfolds within the vertigo of the antipodes and between the magnetic planes they irradiate. But those poles where the curved lines of magnetization coincide are not the poles of Manichean gnosticism: Bataille's antipodes are not opposing principles of a single *whole*, because if such were the case they would constitute unity a priori; rather, they are *wholes* that follow one after the other because they cannot coexist. Toward *awakening*, toward Breton's "spiritual point" (point of fusion), enemy spheres revolve in thought. The point where all magnetic curves blur and *loving antipodes* unite: ananda.[7]

A reading that found in this dualism the translation of certain Oriental philosophies would not be in error: Manicheanism was saturated with them. It would be riskier to claim that Bataille's passion for binaries introduced to Western thought the pair of opposites central to Taoism: that of the *yin* and the *yang*.[8] The *yin*, "principle of shadow, cold, femininity, invites our withdrawal, rest, *passivity*"; the *yang*, "principle of light, heat, and masculinity incites the expenditure of energy, activity, and even aggressiveness."[9] At the point of fusion, there is only one binary notion missing: sacred-profane. Sacredness, as Hollier points out, is precisely that fusion with its opposite. Prior to the definitive abolition of opposites, only transgression creates the continual step from one sphere to the other. From Evil (a space that is also limited and to which any "fidelity" would be impossible) the new transgression (the betrayal of Evil) returns us to the sphere of Good. To betray betrayal, transgress transgression: the only "grace."

The Three Transgressions

Here a marginal reflection intrudes: of thought's three transgressions as discussed by Bataille (thought itself, eroticism, and death), I believe that only one, the first, continues to exist with its original force. Bourgeois society (especially that society which does not admit to being bourgeois) has mitigated the resistance inspired in it by eroticism and death in order to intensify, to a pathological degree, its resistance to self-reflective thought. Blasphemy, homosexuality, incest, sadism, and death are now relatively well-tolerated transgressions. (I am not talking about the childish transgression of "protest art": bourgeois thought is not merely unperturbed, it is pleased by the representation of the bourgeoisie as exploitation, of capitalism as decay.) The one thing the bourgeoisie will not tolerate, what really drives it crazy, is the idea that *thought can think about thought*, that *language can talk about language*, that an author *does not write about something but writes something*, as Joyce said. Faced with this transgression, which for Bataille was the meaning of *awakening*, believers and atheists, capitalists and communists, aristocrats and proletarians, readers of Mauriac and of Sartre find themselves suddenly and definitively in agreement. The distrust and aggressiveness provoked by current critical theories illustrate the *unity* that exists among the most opposing ideologies when faced with the truth of Bataille's *awakening*.

MARMORI

Empty Signs

Before pointing out the place that echoes of the final image from *Les Larmes d'Éros* have occupied in two Latin American narratives, I would like to attempt a commentary on something that strikes me as a radical inversion in the diachrony of writing in the tradition of Sade.

The five "active" characters of Giancarlo Marmori's *Storia di Vous* (Olivia and Si, who signify the plan, the intelligence of the sadistic act; Suzana, whose mediation and skill allow it to be carried out; Brother, who sponsors the sacrificial ceremony; and Domenico, who is the complicitous gaze) build on the Void. As François Wahl explains, Vous, the protagonist, is "progressively dispossessed of her body, which is transformed little by little into a *thing* by the strange ornaments that are gradually encrusted on it, making it impossible for her to move at all." The reification of the other, and its fixity, are already present in this definition: the hypothetical certainty of the sadistic space. Everything works to reiterate this for us: the "perverse" relationships among the women, the glacial execution of their gestures, the sexual connotation of their postures.

Only one detail serves to alter, to belie the sadistic configuration from within, creating through its withdrawal the impression of a structure with a void at the center: in *Storia di Vous* there is not a single sign, explicit or otherwise, of resistance to suffering. Moreover: during the entire story Vous "suffers" her transformation into a jewel without speaking a single word (except on one of the last pages where she says, precisely, "Vous"), submitting without a complaint in the totality of her *yin* as if language, a foreign attitude, belonged essentially to the sphere of aggression, activity—the *yang*—, as if the third person (Si) signified this opposition in its antipodal relation to the second (Vous).

For her first appearance Vous surrenders herself as artificiality and animalness, the hypostasis of the accessory that will be transformed, slowly, into the essential: "Her face was made up violently, her mouth painted with branches. Her eye sockets were black and painted with alumina: they were narrow between her eyes and then extended by whorls, paint, and powdered metal in wide borders and arabesques—like swans' eyes, but in richer and more varied colors—all the way to her temples and the base of her nose; instead of lashes, a fringe of gaudy artificial jewelery hung from her eyelids. From feet to neck, Vous was a woman; above, her body was transformed into a kind of heraldic animal with a baroque snout."

The officiants, the goldsmiths, will keep adorning, encrusting her with strange jewels, setting her with stones and metals, until she is immobile, asphyxiated.

The ceremony has no meaning other than the horror of the void, the confused proliferation of signs, the reduction of a body to a baroque fetish that from "an inverted oblong **Y** decorated with a few branches climbing across its belly" finally becomes something odious because of so many additions, settings (her entire body is now encrusted; a small transparent globe is soldered to her sex): "*'There's too much on her!'* Olivia exclaimed. . . . Vous's forehead was graced with a branch of feathers, a mounted bouquet of fluffy tassels, a tufted horn between her eyes."

Modern Style

The rhetoric of the accessory becoming the essential, the proliferation of adjectivals as substantives, excessive ornamentation, contortion, stylized vegetation, statues and swans, cosmetics as instruments of restrained sadism, place us, as Marmori demonstrates in *Le Vergini Funeste*, in a precise eroticism: the eroticism celebrated in borders and body metaphors by 1900 art.

The story of Vous could also be read as a ceremony in which "the vials, sprinklers, eyebrow pencils, and paintbrushes are equivalent to censers and chalices." Marmori enlarges and clarifies the obscure rite of ornamentation, of disguise. Venus before the mirror. But a Venus who receives neither her own image nor the gaze of her servants. How can one help thinking of *La Toilette de Salomé*, that drawing by Aubrey Beardsley of which Vous's passion could be the literary double, the textual conversion?

Passive before her mirror, breast bared, head lowered, Vous-Salomé submits to the cosmetic ceremony. Nothing distracts her from that submission: neither her image nor the vases with oriental designs nor the strange decorations and flowers that surround her. She closes her eyes while a solicitous masked figure, an enormous cat (Brother), looks for a place to stick a flower in her hair or, perhaps, with an effeminate gesture, removes a white speck with his fingertips. A smiling, naked hermaphrodite (Domenico or Suzana) approaches with a tray. Two women—one of whom, seated on a hexagon covered with oriental designs, is naked except for a large bracelet and elfin slippers, and the other is standing, wrapped in a blanket (Olivia and Si)—soberly maintain the absorption characteristic of spectators at a ceremony.

In her metamorphosis, Vous will first become one of Gustave Klimt's "ominous" women. Her face and hands are the only parts of her body that protrude from the oppressive plaque formed by the proliferation of exotic jewelry, Byazantine golds, brooches with Egyptian eyes, metal fish, flowers. Neither Alfonse Mucha's Maga nor Gustave Moreau's Salomé, for all their ornamental frenzy, achieves the plating, the precise imbrication that makes Klimt's muses so static. Prisoners in their baroque niches, "*murate vive*," *fixed*.

The phantom of fixity is present in both Klimt and Marmori. Like the Judith of 1901, Vous is reduced to a statue, reified. But here, as in Georges de Feure's fairy tales, it is lianas, laces, and flowers—metaphorical cords—that imprison. The object-acts undergo the mediation of painting-makeup, of metalwork-encrustration.

The final image of Vous, "on the hill, alone, in the exclamation of her body," which is that of a luminous object, an anthropomorphic jewel, but also, in a certain way, that of a martyr, a Christ-female (in Elizondo we will see the coincidence of this image with another that might be called a counterimage), has no equivalent in the sadistic-ornamental iconography of 1900 art. The metalization, the *aurification* of Vous[10] has no parallel other than the bodies tattooed with arabesques, encrusted inch by inch with stones, feathers, birds' heads (the bodies themselves are birds' heads), flower-sexes in Svanberg's paintings. *Bouquets de Lumière et de Crépuscule* is the visual double, the conversion of Vous's last stage into painting, just as her first stage converted *La Toilette de Salomé* into literature. Painting converted into text, which is converted into painting. Pleated colors, chromatic letters, and no unembellished discourse. Unlike traditional critics, who are imprisoned by their own notions and afraid to apply the adjective *literary* to great painting, I believe that the *graphy* of Beardsley and Svanberg, like Leonor Fini's figures, which are absent in their literal presence, can be included in the category of text. In the same way, writing—Marmori's conjuring—creates on the page a space of pure plasticity that is systematized by perspectives, exists only when a glance passes across it, and causes us to exist only when it glances at us.

From the mirror that begins the ceremony until the final splendor of the funereal jewels that asphyxiate Vous-Christ, Marmori's writing unfolds in the theater of physical rituals, the sequence of doors-arches-borders that expose a naked body to death.

CORTÁZAR

The Double

The value of inversion discussed by Bataille, the circle where torture and ecstasy coincide, may now be discussed in several works (which it is possible to group under the same heading only on the basis of this metaphoric cordon) so as to exclude them from such a circle or, on the contrary, to enclose them within its compass.

One of José Gutiérrez Solana's paintings reproduces a photograph of the Leng Tch'e. The painter's manifest art is not limited to copying, which would emphasize (especially, perhaps, in the case of a photograph) the triviality of his exercise, but, rather, "interprets," connotes his reproduction of the document with adjectives drawn from our morality. Here, in the painting, everything has fallen into place: displaying their cruelty (their faces are officially sadistic, treacherous, and sardonic; one of them puffs absent-mindedly on his pipe), the executioners are recovered by the Spanish expressionist tradition, as if the images were refuting chance. The wasted victim assumes his role as martyr without reticence, brandishes his suffering. In Gutiérrez Solana's "translation," the document has lost the cathartic force which makes possible ambiguity, breach, and which allowed Bataille to see an expression of happiness on the victim's face. In his interpretation, the painter has trembled for us, suffered for us, using the signs of torture to connote something whose torturous power consists precisely in its occurrence as pure denotation.

The result is quite different when these photographs are inserted—described—in Chapter 14 of *Rayuela* (*Hopscotch*). They turn up in Wong's hands; he carries them in his wallet, and one night when the "club" holds a meeting, he shows them to Oliveira. In this description, the narrator introduces several variations that provide a gauge of the distance Cortázar establishes between himself and the narrator of *Hopscotch*: Wong's pictures were taken with a "1920 Kodak" by some "North American or Danish ethnologist" and there is a woman in them; Bataille's pictures were taken in 1905 by a French photographer and (unless Elizondo's interpretation is correct) no woman appears.

It would be interesting if we could locate that fact on the topology of the narration, which may not be possible without effecting certain reductions. The first is this: *Hopscotch* is a novel about the subject. Oliveira's search (for gnoseological totality) is a search for the subject's unity. But writing about the *subject* is writing about *language*, which is to say, thinking about the relation or coincidence of the two, knowing that the space of one is the space of the other, that language is never (as Sartre believed) just a *practico-inert* used by the subject to express itself, because, on the contrary, the subject is what constitutes language—or, if you prefer, both are illusory.

In any case, an exploration of the subject is an exploration of language. For this reason, *Hopscotch* is about language—its plot and apparent discontinuity take place only within language, with no referent other than the sentence. This discontinuity is the analogy of phonetic *discretion* and also of the leap between Heaven and Earth made by another system of signs, another graphic code: hopscotch.[†] A reading of squares chalked on the sidewalk, a reading of sentences, novels: discontinuity, leap.

In relation to the realm of language, the novel's story and the hopscotch figure on the sidewalk are equally external (neither of these referents is antecedent; their only truth is their telling, their encounter on the page), and within that realm a structure of doubles is gradually established.

If we consider only the main characters, it will seem that La Maga (or perhaps La Maga-Talita) signifies ignorance-knowledge. La Maga knows nothing, her life is a continual question, her novelistic emblem a question mark. But this inclination causes the reversal of her ignorance, as if asking were the answer par excellence. La Maga's magic, in other words her essence, is her wisdom. Instinctively, she knows everything, not intellectually but mantically, not through information but by intuition. *Her not knowing is a trompe-l'oeil.* Oliveira (or perhaps Oliveira-Traveler) is on the other side of the coin: knowledge-ignorance.

Perverse Miracles

In his incomplete world, in his thirst for wholeness, Oliveira is aware of the limitations in our way of thinking: "'Western dichotomies,' Oliviera said. 'Life and death, the here below and the hereafter.'"

In that vast scheme of limitations only Wong seems to possess truly vast knowledge ("Listen to me, sit here and you'll learn

[†]"Heaven is at the top, Earth is on the bottom, . . . one day you learn how to leave Earth and get the pebble soaring up to Heaven. . . ." (Julio Cortázar, *Rayuela* [Buenos Aires: Editorial Sudamericana, 1969] 251). *Rayuela* has been translated into English by Gregory Rabassa (*Hopscotch* New York: Pantheon, 1966). *Translator's note.*

about things even Wong doesn't know") or perhaps even the ability to guess which people could overcome limitations ("'Wong has subjected me to various "tests",' Ronald explained. 'He says I'm smart enough to start destroying my intelligence profitably. We've agreed that I'll read the Bard carefully, and from there we'll progress to the basic stages of Buddhism.'").

Wong's is the only philosophical position not explicitly present in the novel (and Wong himself is a totally marginal character): the one that introduces an empty reference into a context where almost all Western philosophical positions are expressed (in the monologues of Étienne, Ronald, Gregorovius, and Oliveira). And it is Wong who occupies the empty space. He is the only one whose position is not marked by the expression of an ideology (or by any expression), the one whose sign is absence, who is continually referred to by the others and is continually silent; he is the bearer of nothingness who owns the array of photographs in which Bataille had found conversion. Like a person who carries medals or prayer cards with him, Wong carries those reverse prayer cards, those icons of perverse miracles "in a wallet made of black leather."(Is it by chance that this sadistic signifier turns up here?)

In order for the access to emptiness, the "path" to pass through the contemplation of torture: this is why such a secondary and apparently displaced character is inserted in a novel about the subject, about wholeness. The insertion is one of photographs or hieroglyphs of the character's knowledge, of that Buddhist "knowledge" about how to become no expression, emptiness.

But neither Chapter 14 nor the novel has an aphoristic value. Only the strangeness of Wong's interruption is explicit, the fact that he and his ideas, and the photographs, appear in *Hopscotch*.

Nothing more is suggested. Perhaps this explains why the *disturbance* of the story caused by the episode with Wong has occasioned so many interpretations: religion and sadism. Conversion.

ELIZONDO

Yin / Yang

Question or answer. A question that is the "posing of an

enigma,'' the ''uttering of a riddle, the repetition of a magic formula.'' An answer ''to an unknown question, a coded inquisition.'' This is how Salvador Elizondo presents the text of his *Farabeuf o La crónica de un instante* (Farabeuf or The Chronicle of an Instant), which explains a double basis for the photograph of the Leng Tch'e: a theoretical basis that related the experience to ''the Chinese method of divination by means of symbolic hexagrams,'' a practical basis since the torture frozen in the photograph is reactivated right in the middle of Paris, in the familiar geography of the Latin Quarter.

Farabeuf's theory is based on an analogous premise: in the photograph, ''the executioners are placed so as to form a hexagon inscribed in the space around an axis that is formed by the victim. This is also the equivocal representation of a Chinese ideogram . . . . it is the number six and is pronounced *liú*. The placement of its lines recalls the victim's position.''

In other words, the entire experience may have been merely the dramatization of an ideogram, perhaps something similar to the splitting of the metaphor represented by all signs, a discovery of the real base hidden behind all signals, of the original reality of ideogrammatic language.

Farabeuf's narrator also thinks by analogy about the process of divination: he discovers a similarity between the *ouija*, the method of divination that employs ''the sliding of a planchette over another larger board painted with letters and numbers'' and ''is considered part of the magic hoard of Western culture,'' and the Chinese method of divination by hexagrams. As it slides, the planchette moves from one edge of the board with a YES to the other edge marked with a NO; the hexagrams are made up of combinations of unbroken and broken lines, *YANG* and *YIN*. The handbook of divination that Farabeuf consults seems to be the *I Ching or The Book of Changes*. If the unbroken lines are superimposed in groups of three, the result is eight trigrams (Ch'ien, Tui, Chên, Sun, K'an, Li, Kên, and K'un), which according to legend were drawn by Fu Hsi, a divine being with a serpent's body who was the first mythic ruler. By superimposing these trigrams on each other two by two the diviner obtains 64. If the hexagrams are arranged in a circle (space-time) and each element is assigned to represent one reality, one being, or *one instant*, between Ch'ien (three *Yang* elements, Heaven) and K'un (three *Yin* elements,

Earth) the hexagrams may be thrown at random and compared so as to interpret them with the help of a commentary and arrive at *Crónica de un instante*.

Certain Sounds

In *Farabeuf*, certain sounds, related to one method of divination or another, produce unbroken or broken elements, *Yang* or *Yin*, *Yes* or *No*.

Three coins falling on a table indicate *Yin* or *Yang*; the sound of "dragging steps or of one object sliding over another and making a sound like dragging steps heard through a wall" may evoke the sliding of the planchette between the YES and NO of the *ouija*.

The steps of Farabeuf the master, who bears the instruments of torture, gradually outline the signs; the falling coins underline them. In this way, the rite is described, the formula repeated, the chronicle written of that instant whose ultimate meaning is death and whose metaphor is the *liú*. Farabeuf's "meticulous" praxis will reverse this metaphor, restore it to its initial literalness.

Sustained on the antipodes, and turning reading into an image of their sequence, *Farabeuf* is the book of sadistic literalness. By making his lover *live* death, by subjecting her to Farabeuf's meticulous surgical technique, by placing her in a theatrical setting he has studied beforehand (one element of which is a mirror), and by comparing her to Christ each time the theoretical, Oriental context seems to distance us, seems to insert the image into the space of distance, of unreality (for Elizondo, the victim in the photograph is a woman: hence his image of a Christ-female), the narrator of *Farabeuf* restores—on the plane of the story, within the space of an instant—that structure whose terms I also found present in some way in texts by Sade, Bataille, Marmori, and Cortázar: eroticism, theater, religion, and death.

Marmori structures sadistic ritual on its signifying level—gestures—in order to belie that level, to create deception on the level of the signified (suffering). He writes the sadistic phrase against the void, a false ideogram: behind its signifying appearance there is nothing; it is pure outline, a gesture that refers only to itself, a meaningless invocation. Elizondo, on the other hand, wants to prove the presence of the signified, prove that every signifier is no more than a rhetorical figure, theater, the writing of an *idea*, in other words, an *ideo-gram*. A jolting of the signifier, in this case the outline of the *liú*, something like a psychoanalysis of the ideogram, should reveal its support, in this case the concept of torture.

The issue here is one of metaphoric philology. What gave rise to graphy, of what reality is every letter a hieroglyphic, what does each sign hide and displace?: those are the questions raised by *Farabeuf*. How would it be possible to create a sentence, an organization of unsupported graphies, a meaningless emblem, a sadistic ritual devoid of suffering?—this was the question raised by *Storia di Vous*.

On both sides of the sign, those inquiries (whose full intent I have not adequately defined in these notes) show that in spite of our resistance we are beginning to explore a plane of literalness previously off limits, formulating the question about our own being, about our *humanity* that first and foremost questions the being of our writing.

A PEARL GRAY CASHMERE FETISH

To create that space which is sacred because the distance between sacred and profane has been abolished; to deny the outside world and assimilate into the warm vegetal cloister where he lives the Mother who dominates him, who magnetizes him with her beauty and terror: in Carlos Fuentes's *Zona sagrada* (Sacred Zone) such is the *passion* of the hero, Mito (the final abbreviation of his name—Guillermo, Guillermito, Mito [Myth]—also describes the substratum of the book—the mythological).[1] The novella might be read as an exposé of a castrating celebrity's maternal hegemony: she is Mexican actress Claudia Nervo, a symbol of Mexico, a Pancho Villa, whose mythology already corresponds to that of a female Valentino. Jacques Vaché's comment would then have to be transvestized: "Rien ne vous tue *une femme* comme d'être obligée de représenter un pays." In addition to considering the work an Oedipus complex served Mexican style, it is also possible to justify other readings:

—the appearance of an undermined language: Fuentes's Spanish, his Mexican are gradually eroded, streaked with French, with Italian, with another parallel syncretic language that eventually becomes everyone's language;

—a novel about a novel: what is "written" in Guillermo, the composition of his life;

—a self-mocking Odyssey whose archeological model, the real Odyssey, is found in the narration;

—an adventure in which the Other is possessed by:
mimesis of the space surrounding him,
destruction of his double,
fetishism,
and transvestism.

A Totem Face

Outside Mito's room, which is the sacred zone that is the sphere of chance and play, irrecoverable, at the center of the rival zone, there is a face. Not one reference to Claudia's hands (might they be excessively human?), to her her body in its opaqueness, in its material presence; only her language, only her function as sign is noted: a linear, resolute, virile wardrobe of brusque gestures, a voice that someone in the commotion made by her fans compares to a sergeant's voice; a firm, rapid gait. Nothing in this body warrants fascination: Claudia Nervo belongs to the imaginary realm of the close-up, her face is a signifier, motionless in its iconic authority, set like a mask, copied, imitated, distorted a thousand times, continually analyzed and reassembled, obsessive, a face that multiplies its inquisitorial gaze, a butterfly imprinted with pupils, a totem.

That face (the aggessive gaze, "its oldest and most powerful weapon," will prevent us from deciphering it) belongs to a former iconographic age, the age of "terror," an age whose advent finds the film industry in full possession of its technique, the age of Valentino and Garbo, an age when "you could literally lose yourself in a human image as if it were a philter, when the face formed something akin to a state of absolute flesh, a state you could neither reach nor relinquish."[2] Like Valentino's and Garbo's, Claudia's face appears in Fuentes's description as an archetype. Claudia is not a figure but a "Platonic idea of the human being"; not a woman, but a concept, a carnal essence, something both defined and neuter at the same time. Neuter, not because her face is sexless, "divine," absent—like Garbo's—, but because in it the sexes meet and do battle. In that "meeting of old ivory and nascent light," in the lunate space of her complexion (*Yin*), "her black eyes are poised, tensed, ready to pounce with claws of highly spontaneous ridicule, anger, or laughter" (*Yang*). That face-object is conceptual through saturation and antagonism, because it sets the sexual antipodes in opposition and abolishes them, and it emphasizes the Caravaggio-like effect of dark eyes superimposed on white skin; because it joins the ethereal with the telluric, the perfect with the ephemeral.

After the age of *terror*, movies entered the age of *charme*, of individualized faces. "As language, Garbo's singularity was conceptual in nature; Audrey Hepburn's is substantial in nature. Garbo's face is Idea; Hepburn's is Event." *Terror* grants Claudia Nervo's face its magnetism, that perfection her son wants to attract, incorporate, abolish, as if to fill his own empty face to which the maternal Other has not delegated her essence.

A Modern Style Temple

In her son's universe, Claudia represents the category of inaccessibility, of refusal, rejection, and expulsion. Since she is unreachable on the plane of reality, Mito, a fallen angel, tries to possess her on the symbolic plane. The sacred zone for his contest is a precinct analogous to the maternal, a chamber to which he can *return*, as though to childhood, to the irrecoverable: a 1900-style jungle modeled on Claudia, on an old photograph of Sarah Bernhardt's apartment, and on *Salomé* as illustrated by Beardsley, a grotto reminiscent of Rubén Darío, covered with scarlet silk, "untied knots, knotted parallels, delicate slender pistils of opaque glass, leaded-glass lamps that are closed flowers and open fruits, curtains of precious stones, marbles, beads, thick strings like rosaries between the living and dining rooms, screens with swans and dancers so thin you can see their ribs. . . ."

Opalescent glasses, iridescent Tiffany metals, Guimard's vegetal ogives, and Lalique's branches crowned with peacocks govern this baroque space, this "unrestrained, curvilinear, flamboyant proliferation" that is feminine in the curve of its lines, maternal in its hermeticism. The sieved light of the sacred zone, filtered by mother-of-pearl and thick glass shades, aims to suggest the light in the mother's house and, metaphorically, that of the womb, "a white light that granulates everything and hunts down the edges until it expels them all, this is what the inside of that first cloister must be like, an illuminated placenta similar to this gallery where all details of decor disappear, dissolved in a humid dust."

Claudia's house, with its furnishings of "open hands, eucharistic goblets, trees of leather and Brazilian rosewood," is now the rival zone, the nebulous model that must be seized. Her son seizes it, like a primitive hunter, by reconstructing its strength-giving image, by winning the symbolic battle first so that later the real battle will be no more than a repetition: "I return here, like the Incas, to renew my energy."

Only the maternal double limits and defines the borders of that "private country": "I drink in my decor of Turkish stools and divans sunk beneath the weight of painted silks and Persian rugs, cushions encrusted with pearls, small, untouchably smooth satin pillows. The cloister envelops me, my weary trembling welcomes it without an edge. . . ."

Layered Imposture

If Claudia's is the archetypal face, no face copies or imitates it better than the face of Bella, an Italian model drawn to Mexico by Nervo's aura. Simulacrum and caricature, Bella's face duplicates for Mito not only his mother's face but also that of the woman who disguised herself as his mother and kidnapped him when he was a child. Equidistant between the mother and the impostor layered with make-up, Bella is a counterfeit of the original, of its essence, and a verification of the mask. The son recognizes himself in her, and at the same time his identification is a denial. As the recovery of a layered imposture and the derision of her model, Bella simultaneously seduces and terrifies, attracts and repels, because her disguise is not offered as a *simile*; on the contrary, like an artist who makes the deed of imitation explicit in his copied canvas, Bella's disguise calls attention to, proclaims its own false nature: "She flaunts her immodesty, her long black hair, which is obviously dyed or perhaps a wig, her arched eyebrows, which are plucked and painted deliberately, imitatively, like the bow of her lips and the fake mole on her cheek."

Aggressive attraction and mocking seduction, Bella is a distorting mirror for Mito, a clownish double of himself: "Disguised as Claudia and then disguised as me." For Mito, who has delegated his narcissism to the face, to that face, his is the only reflection, the only mimesis of Claudia.

Claudia is surrounded by a feminine court—emblem women—, which Fuentes has made somewhat hieratic: Vanessa, the minstrel; Ute, the virgin; Hermione, the cop; Kirsten, the martyr; Paola, the angel; Ifigenia, the totem; and Bella, the new arrival, the best imitation. Among these signs, only Claudia's face is an absence of codes, convention, nature. A human among phantoms, Fuentes says, she was painted by Leonora Carrington. (I imagine her, a human among signs, painted by Leonor Fini.) For Mito, Claudia's court represents sarcasm, grimace. By copying her face, Bella-kidnapper is "denying all (her) singularities, invading (her) personality, mocking (her) identity."

The phantom of the destroyed mirror intervenes here as demystification, denunciation. By destroying Bella, destroying in Bella what resembles Claudia and therefore resembles him, the son vindicates himself as the absolute analogy, as the sole image of his mother: "I throw myself on Bella, pause before her happy merciless gaze, raise my hand and let it fall on those layers of false paint. . . ."

In that action there is a reduction (inverted) and a theatrical premise, of the transvestism at the novella's end. Before he actually turns into his mother, or her credible double, the son destroys the disguise, the intrusion between her image and the mirror.

Freedom and Constraint

If, as the narrative progresses, the sweater that Mito steals from his mother is gradually transformed until it is finally invested with the grandeur of a relic; if that object gradually comes to stand out from the surface of fictional transformations until it becomes a *center of permutations*, that is because it fulfills its erotic role as fetish: "*it is spatially delimited, immutable, one might say 'firm,' consistent with itself, free of physical fluctuation, in short, transcendent.*"[3] In order for it to assume the characteristics of a "painful object" on the symbolic plane, Mito—sure of being humiliated and punished—returns the sweater to his mother soiled, "just like a rag"; in order to have it "*become devalued, provoke repulsion,*" it is given to (and then stolen back from) his maid, who in turn loans it to her lover.

As an extension of his mother's body and an object that has been used to cover it, the sweater will follow the "*metaphoric-metonymic oscillation*" of all fetishes: it is a metonymic object because it is "a part, a simple extension of the maternal body, the woof of the screen that covers her, the felt of her clothing"; it is a metaphoric object because "in no way, not even in shape, does it suggest the penis," the ultimate base of all fetishism. All of these laws are found, so to speak, in their textual precision in Fuentes's novella, since here not even another woman replaces the mother; the narcissism that supports the entire fetishist mechanism is also explicit in the *analogy,* in the *credible double* mentioned above. When Claudia refuses to take back her sweater, the ensuing disappointment takes the form of depression:

"Don't argue anymore. Keep it.

I pick up the sweater. This time, it's meaningless to press it against my chest, to inhale its scent with my eyes closed. This time, it's useless."

The return of the sweater (when Mito goes into the maid's room and leaves it on the dresser) prefigures the guilty return to the mother's house; in other words, in the space of transgression, far from being depressing, deceptive, the fetish plays out its role with respect to the "narcissistic 'erection' that supports it." "I must caress the sweater one more time and remember how I took it from my mother's closet and how I fell asleep with its soft fuzz next to my cheek. How I kept it for a whole month under my pillow where I could always reach it. Now I give it up forever. Not without kissing it first, for the last time, closing my eyes and realizing that none of its original fragrance lingers any longer."

Once the sweater has become, from the excess of fetishist contemplation, the novella's central object, it participates in a series of permutations, which guide the thread of the narrative, the physiology of the novella, and which could even be formalized almost mathematically in a diagram:

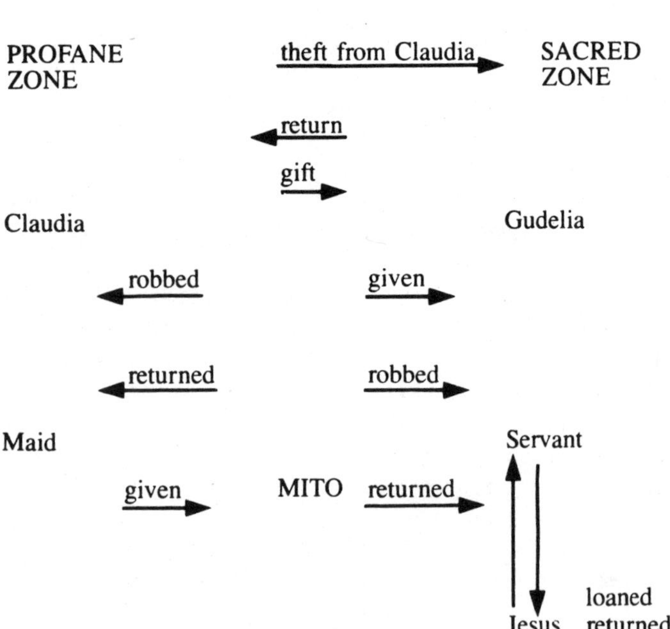

Invested with its immunity as a fetish, the sweater travels from the profane to the sacred, returns, and begins the cycle again. When its roles are studied from a formal point of view, it is evident that even within the two zones, the object-fetish describes analogous, symmetrical structures:

The return in which the fetish becomes an object of arousal occurs on the *outside of the inside*, in other words in Gudelia's room, the only place in Mito's apartment where his presence is experienced as an intrusion: the return in which the fetish becomes an object of depression occurs in the *inside of the outside*, in other words, in Claudia's room, the only place in her apartment where Mito's presence is tolerated (he has been expelled like an intruder from the rest of the house where a cocktail party is in progress: Claudia hates to admit publicly that she has a son of his age).

If Fuentes's work constructs a myth from real elements, no element bears its transpositon better than the sweater. Superimposed on the narrative surface, endowed with the hallucinatory relief found in certain objects of Magritte and Pop Art, the pearl gray cashmere fetish explicitly becomes the support of some totally codified constraints: "The production of meaning is subject to certain constraints, which is to say that constraints do not limit meaning but, on the contrary, constitute it; meaning cannot arise where freedom is total or nonexistent: meaning's rules are those of a supervised freedom."[4]

In its bivalence, which is thematic (fetishism) and structural (a hub of activity), the sweater in *Zona sagrada* illustrates that dialectic of meaning and code, freedom and constraint.

A Change of Skin

The apotheosis of contiguity—clothing as body, a woof that, like the covered object, instructs by covering—, in other words the apotheosis of the accessory, will take place in the chapter that concludes the novella and signifies it thematically; in his mother's closed-up house, and before the mirrors of her dressing room—an empty theater—Mito celebrates the ceremony of disguise, the ritual of transformation. The fascination of the fetish-object extends metonymically to all objects, the spell of the sweater to everything that has touched Claudia's body: "Then, letting myself go with increasing pleasure, voluptuously, sinking into clothes, coats, foxes, and ermines, and chinchillas that still smell of her perfume, the scent of my kidnapping, the perfume of my childhood. Finally, sitting on the floor among her shoes, which I also caress, which I also press against my cheek and my eyes, which I also kiss. . . ." But the exaltation of metonymy is also its inversion: from a worshipper of everything that has touched Claudia's body, Mito wants to become Claudia by surrounding himself with everything that has touched her body. To worship the Other is to become the Other. "Surrounded by her objects, I understand; she lets me see myself as something different; she lets me see myself as her."

As with the pope in Brecht's *Galileo*, who gradually assumes his authority, his veracity, while he dresses, so for Mito the rite of transvestism gradually returns him to himself, to the recovery of his image: "I'll rummage in the bureau; everything I want is here; the brassiere I fasten behind, the lace panties, black stockings, garters, trinkets, her jade rings, her aquamarine earrings, the amethyst necklace, the silver bracelets, another topaz necklace."

Just as an officiant accepts the instruments of sacred pantomime with prescribed gestures, so Mito gradually accepts on his body the maternal attributes, the adjectiving of the Other, the fetishes of conversion and femininity. Here, as in the 1900 art that initiated this parable of possession, what is accessory is essential; things added to the body are its signs; false elements, its condition. Mito is Claudia insofar as he is the support of her finery. Sardonic but subdued by the intensity of Mito's transgression, the objects now begin to appear which metamorphosis will slowly steal from triviality, rescue from their death as *things*, from their *artifice* in order to convert them into *nature*, into truth. "Her wig. Her eyebrow pencil. Her eyeshadow. Her false eyelashes. The beauty mark from her cheek. The lipstick. The Hindu bracelet, the golden snake."

In disguise there is an implicit worship of the Other; in conversion through transvestism, a conjuring to make the Other disappear, an exorcism that demands death: while Claudia is alive, while the model, the archetypal face is present (omnipresent in its totemic authority), all conversion is useless, all metamorphosis ridiculous. While Claudia is alive, Mito disguised as Claudia will be likened to the kidnapper's imposture, to layers of makeup, to "a prince of jesters, a puppet smeared with cosmetics, a Christmas tree decked with cheap jewelry, a starving dog that can no longer stand up on its high heels, its towering stilts."

The final clauses of the sequence formulate the vow of extermination. Now it is Claudia who usurps an identity, who copies her son. The essence has been corrupted, the face-archetype is a falsification: the witch must disappear so Mito can take her place, her identity, relive her life and perhaps father another son so the cycle can begin anew.

Another "Sacred Zone"

Over the circle of erotic possessions, "Sacred Zone" traces another circle, metaphors of possession: seizing the beloved object by reproducing the space that surrounds it, destroying its double, creating a fetishist relationship. This succession of desire and object desired is endless, even when the desirer becomes what he desires; his only goal is perhaps death, the obliteration of the desired object. Fuentes depicts the persistent imbalance of reality and desire, the irrecoverable distance between object and ghost, the trace left by a body as it disappears.

Starting from another, apparent (structural) inversion, his book elucidates a real (sexual) inversion.

If we believed that the intelligibility of literature was to be found outside of literature (in this case in psychoanalysis), that a text could be deciphered on the basis of its referents, we would assert that "Sacred Zone" inverts fetishism's normal topology, that the *zones* have been subjected to a permutation, a reciprocal displacement that lets the narrative work. In fact, according to the extraliterary information given above, the theft of the sweater should have occurred in the opposite direction; the space surrounding the mother should have been the sacred zone, not the area around the son. In that way, theft as a ritual incorporation of something belonging to the sacred would have its full "scientific" coherence. But Fuentes has switched the planes, as if he wanted to show us that literary discourse tows scientific contents but that these contents are significant only insofar as they articulate the twists of the plot and become one of its games, one of its figures. This involves a simulacrum, mimetic activity, subject matter analogous to scientific material, although in discourse that double is no longer science but science converted into literature.[5]

In this way Fuentes confirms the autonomy of the esthetic process and uses words to sketch the limits of that other zone (which is also sacred because it assimilates and converts into its own substance everything that passes through it), the zone of literature, of the inexhaustible symbolic production of language.

WRITING / TRANSVESTISM

Although restrained, there is an outcrop of mockery in the reverence and mastery of Goya's portraits. Burlesque, the compulsive force of the ridiculous, seems to break up his canvas; it undermines the expressive majesty of those ladies of the Spanish court and turns them into serene grotesques.

If we are moved, simultaneously, to respect and derision, piety and laughter as we look at those figures, it is because something about the royal panoply that defines them points out its own *sham*. I am of course referring to the plump, bejeweled María Luisa in *The Family of Charles IV* whose coiffure is pierced by a diamond arrow, and especially to the Marquesa de Solana, who is crowned with an enormous pink felt feather. *Without resorting to a visible alteration of forms*, the sham in those royal witnesses slyly changes jewels to junk, finery to disguise, smiles to grimaces.

I venture these references to Goya because they are exemplified so well by Manuela, the heroine of José Donoso's *El lugar sin límites* (The Place That Hath No Limits). In Manuela—both queen and scarecrow—an outcrop of something false points to the abomination of a *postiche*; the portrait turns into a blot, the drawing becomes a smudge, for this character is a transvestite, a person who has carried the experience of inversion to the limit.

The Goyesque element in Manuela irrupts when Manuel González Astica suddenly makes his appearance on the level of gestures, of feminine-gendered phrases, but *without resorting to a visible alteration of* (grammatical) *forms*. "Skinny as a broomstick, with long hair and eyes that are almost as made-up as the eyes of the Farías sisters" (fat harpists), Manuel is a dancer who once came to the village to liven up a party at Japonesa's brothel, where his performance in a "theatrical" with the madam made him a father.

Russian Dolls

The central inversion, Manuel's, initiates a series of inversions, whose sequence provides the novel's structure. In this sense *El lugar sin límites* continues the mythic tradition of the "world turned upside down," which was practiced so diligently by the surrealists. More than transvestism—in other words, the outward appearance of sexual inversion—the novel's meaning is inversion itself: a metonymic chain of "upsets," of transposed dénouements, controls the narrative progression.

Manuela, who novelistically (grammatically) *signifies* that he is a woman—the first inversion—*performs* as a man since as a man he attracts Japonesa. This attraction leads the curious madame to stage the "theatrical": her motive (the village landowner promises her a house if she provides him with a bit of that lavish drama and manages to arouse the apocryphal dancer) is only a pretext, the pretext used by money to justify all transgressions.

Another inversion occurs within this one: in the sexual act Manuela, who is defined as a man by narrative authority, plays the passive role. Not the feminine role—consequently there is one inversion within another and not simply a return to the original transvestism—, but that of a passive man who fathers a child in spite of himself. Japonesa possesses him by making him possess her. She is the active element of the *act* (active also with respect to the "theatrical": merely one glance is enough to create the space of performance, to establish the Other, the scene). This series of *adjustments*, the metaphor of the Russian doll, could be diagramed.

Inversions:

1st a man dresses as a woman
↓
2nd who attracts because of the man in her
↓
3rd who is *passive* in the sexual act

This formal chain that structures and plots the coordinates of the narrative space is "reflected" thematically on the affective level. The repulsion provided by the grotesque changes into attraction: Pancho Vega, the hamlet's official macho, pursues Manuela because in spite (or because) of all the prohibitions he is fascinated by her mask, her Goyesque imposture. The final sadistic act, perpetrated by Pancho and his underling Octavio, is a substitute for possession. Incapable of confronting his own desire, of assuming the image of himself imposed by that desire, the macho—a transvestite in reverse—becomes an inquisitor, an executioner.

Donoso skillfully disguises his sentences, masking them as if to place them symbolically within Manuela's affective range, so as—by making the third person work undercover—to assign Manuela "responsibility" for the story, to make her a sneaky "I" on the lookout, the real subject of the enunciation: the entire *he/she* is a false front; a latent *I* threatens, undermines, cracks it. As in dreams, that other place where there are no limits, everything here says *I*.

Verbs with an agressive meaning (*kick, hit*) are "dubbed" with others that have a sexual connotation (*pant*), with metaphors of desire (the men are "hungry"), penetration ("their hard, drooling bodies wounding his"), pleasure ("their hot bodies writhing"). Finally, as if the underground discourse became perceptible, one phrase makes sadistic glee explicit: "taking pleasure even in the throes of such painful confusion."

Another inversion takes place on the social plane: Japonesita, the current madam at the brothel, is a virgin, and, as if to emphasize that in this inverted world the only possible attraction is caused by disguise, no one desires her.

This game of "upsets" I have described could be extended to the entire narrative mechanism: Donoso substitutes the inversion-within-the inversion for the fictional device of the tale-within-the-tale. This series of twists with turns, however, never provides an image analogous to that of "the world right-side-up" but continually extends its revolution, because what is inverted in each instance is not the entire surface—economics, politics, class tensions are not included in the twists of the plot, and they always correspond to "reality"—, but only its continually changing erotic signifiers, certain verbal planes, the topology defined by certain words.

The *place that hath no limits* is that space of conversions, of transformations and disguises: the space of language.

Appearances Are Deceiving

What deceives us are the elements that make up literature's supposed exteriority—the page, blank spaces and all that emerges from them between the lines, the horizontality of writing itself, etc. This appearance, this unfurling of—and through—visual signifiers (or *graphies*), which in our tradition are phonetic, and the relation created between those signifiers in that privileged place of relation formed by the *plane* of the page, the *volume* of the book, are what persistent prejudice has considered the external aspect of literature, the obverse of something that would be whatever its external aspect *expressed*: content, ideas, messages, or else "fiction," an imaginary world, etc.

Declared or not, the prejudice, sweetened by different vocabularies and adopted by successive dialectics, is the prejudice of realism. Everything about it, about its vast grammar upheld by culture, the guarantee of its ideology, assumes a *reality* outside the text, outside the literalness of writing. That reality, which the author must limit himself to expressing, translating, directs the movement of the page, its body, its languages, the substance of writing. The most naîve readers assume this is the reality of the "the world around us," the reality of events; more astute readers displace that deceit in order to propose an imaginary entity, something fictitious, a "fantastic world." But it is all the same: pure realists—socialists or not—and "magical" realists promulgate and refer to the same myth. A myth rooted in logocentric, Aristotelian knowledge, in the knowledge of an *original*, or something primitive and *true* that the author supposedly brings to the blank page.[1] The creation of a fetish from the new bard, the new demiurge recovered by Romanticism corresponds to this mythic knowledge.

The progress in literary theory made by certain studies and the complete about-face that those studies have occasioned in literary criticism have made us reevaluate what used to be considered the outside, the appearance:

—The unconscious considered a language and subjected to its own rhetorical laws, its codes, and transgressions; the attention paid to signifiers, which create an *effect* that is their meaning, and to the explicit subject matter of dreams (Lacan).

—The "content" of a work considered an absence, metaphors considered signs devoid of content, since it is "that distance from the signified which the symbolic process designates" (Barthes).

The text's apparent exteriority, its surface, its *mask* deceives us, "for if there is a mask there is nothing behind it; a surface that hides nothing more that itself; a surface that prevents us from considering it surface because it leads us to assume there is something behind it. The mask leads us to believe there is depth, but what the mask masks is itself: the mask simulates dissimulation in order to dissimulate that it is only simulation."[2]

Transvestism, as practiced in Donoso's novel, may well be the best metaphor for writing: what Manuela makes us see is not a woman who might be hiding a man *beneath her appearance*, a cosmetic mask, which, if it fell, would reveal a beard, a hard crushed face, but *the very fact of transvestism itself*. No one is unaware—given the obviousness of his disguise and the transparency of his artifice, no one could possibly be unaware—that Manuela is a worn-out dancer, a man in drag, a Goyesque *capricho*. What Manuela presents is the coexistence of masculine and feminine signifiers in a single body: the tension, the repulsion, the antagonism created between them. By means of symbolic language,[3] what Donoso's character signifies is layered make-up, concealment, hiding. Painted eyebrows and a beard, his mask masks its masking: such is the "reality" (one that has no limits since it contaminates everything) that this hero *enunciates*.

Those planes of intersexuality are analogous to the planes of intertexuality that make up the literary object. They are planes conversing in the same exterior, answering and completing, exalting and defining each other: that interaction of linguistic textures, of discourses, that dance, that parody, is writing.

THE (TEXTUAL) ADVENTURE OF A COLLECTOR OF (HUMAN) SKINS

It would be useless to begin with a definition from Littré's dictionary if we wanted to decipher Maurice Roche's *Compact* on the basis of its title.[1] *Compact*, according to that *mémoire* of language, is *the name given to certain conventions established with the Pope or confirmed by him*. In this novel nothing evokes His Holiness: nothing evokes, not even to make fun of it, a *referent* outside the book itself.

Instead, we would find the most appropriate paragram for our reading in the binary opposition *compact/diffuse* employed by Jakobson. Jakobson reminds us that phonologically the notions *compact/diffuse* signify "acoustically—an increased (or, on the contrary, a decreased) concentration of energy in a relatively narrow, central, area of the spectrum, accompanied by a development (or, on the contrary, a diminuition) of the total amount of energy and its expansion in time."[2] In the final analysis, the *"concentration of energy"* comprises the novel's real meaning. The concentration is accomplished phonetically, of course, but also semantically; only a few stylistic devices are used to achieve the message and its development in the book. In these pages everything is *tension*, everything participates in the book's expressive movement: discourse, phrases, words, even the typography itself.

In this sense, *Compact* is a book about the physical. About the physical reality of literature, which is to say the pages whose blankness is underlined literally, and the signs, which unfold in their vast variety, from musical notation to writing in Braille, from pirates' signatures to contemporary advertising. *Compact* emphasizes the signifiers, the physical, voiced aspects of its message, for when the other side of the message is read, when the message is read as the signified, it is also about a body: the book's principal allusion is to *a body*.

The "story" is as follows: In a city (an imaginary city in an unidentified location where every language is spoken), a blind man is dying. A skin collector, who is also a Japanese doctor, and his assistant, a gaudy transvestite, buy the sick man's skin. Their waiting forms the book's plot, the fiction that turns the blind man's tattoos (real or not) into metaphors. While the blind man dies, or rather as he sees death draw closer and closer (yes, of course, as we might have guessed, the blind man is a seer), and as he welcomes it with pithy baroque sentences that are at once profound and parodic, the Japanese and the transvestite hover about him coveting their parchment-like trophy: the exquisite textures of his hide, which are covered with inscriptions embellished with pictograms and hieroglyphs from all ages.

An "Opéra Buffa"

If on the one hand we have a reference to the body and on the other an insistence on signifiers, it is not by chance that we soon find ourselves facing an art that is a catalogue of signifiers by definition, an art that exploits the body in every way possible: the opera.

Philippe Sollers points this out in his preface to *Compact*: the book is constructed like a score for four voices. It is an opera whose theme would be a myth, a progressive fall into blackness, blindness, but at the same time into sight, a story whose *actants* are the personal pronouns, those "persons" that for Sollers are the *you* (singular or plural, familiar or formal) of the reader; the *he* of the Japanese doctor; the *I* or *we* of the blindman who is the subject of the enunciation; and, finally, an empty person, marked by its absence: the absence of everything that, grammatically, is signified by the impersonal.

But if *Compact* is constructed like an opera, if rhetorically these pages are arranged like a score—Maurice Roche is also a musician—, this novel adds a new dimension to the space, the eloquence of the opera: the dimension of parody.[3] *Compact* is an opera that mocks itself, that calls into question all the expressive possibilities available to opera: if we find a certain lyricism ("and the birds under the eaves . . ."), we also find that lyricism mocked ("There was a sparrow pecking in varied rhythms. I listened to his message, in Morse code, pecking at my mental inventories"). The songs, the arias, will be interrupted, undermined by comic turns, by "guttural shrieks" that spring from other textual surfaces, other literary spaces, other languages, and thus from a *duet* with the principal texts, with the melodic line, with the opera's narrative thread.

Writing: Tattooing

There is no code more nebulous than that of everyday communication; nothing more *diffuse* than current language (money). *Compact* represents the pulverization of, the antidote for that single, monochordous, monologic line, for information. To the stupid practice that turns poetry—literature—into the *analogon* of informational language, to soothing *conversational poetry*, *Compact* opposes the domineering request of the signifier, the statue of the text, of literature as an art that is not communicative, that refers only to the *literarity* discussed by the Russian Formalists.

Like the art practiced by our collector, literature is an art of tattooing; within the amorphous mass of informational language it inscribes, encodes the true signs of signification. But this inscription is not possible without wounding, without loss. In order for informational mass to become text, for words to communicate, the writer must tattoo that mass, insert his pictograms in it. Writing could be the art of those *graphies* of discourse appropriating the pictorial, but also the art of proliferation. The bonds between the plastic arts and the written sign as well as its baroque character are present in all literature that retains its *inscriptive* nature, what we could call its *scripturality*.

The Book of the Future

It may be that *Compact* is not an isolated event but one of the inaugural works of a new literature in which language will be present as the space of the *act of encoding,* as a surface of unlimited transformations. Transvestism, the continual metamorphosis of characters, references to other cultures, the mixture of languages, the division of the book in registers (or voices) would all, through their exaltation of the body—dance, gestures, every possible somatic signifier—be the characteristics of that writing. The Carnival, the *Circus*—which is the title of a more recent book by Maurice Roche—, and erotic theater would be the privileged places where fiction could unfold. Beyond censure, beyond common thought, in this scene of writing all former and contemporary texts of the book would converse, all the *translations* that exist within a single language would become explicit. This would be a literature in which all currents, not of thought but of the language that thinks us, would become visible, would confront their textures within the scope of the page.

Compact is one of the books creating that new space, that fiction of the body, of gestures, of eroticism, and of death.

HORROR OF THE VOID

GÓNGORA: SQUARING METAPHOR

Metaphor is that zone where the texture of language thickens, that higher relief in which the remainder of the sentence is returned to its original simplicity, its innocence. A leavening, the flip side of the continuous surface of discourse, metaphors force everything around them to remain in denotative purity. Purity. The moral implications of that word must not be forgotten: because of them metaphors have been considered extrinsic to "natural" language, a "disease"; because of them metaphors have been censured, and the blame has been carried over to all rhetorical figures. No wonder Saint Thomas boasted that he never used any.

But if until Góngora's time metaphors depraved "natural" language, Góngora exonerated rhetoric to such an extreme that in his poetry the first level of what is enunciated, linear, and "healthy," disappears. His point of departure is a terrain eroded, eaten away a priori: the terrain of traditionally poetic metaphors, which for other poets and for literary language are metaphorical discoveries. Góngora starts from that plane—as others start from the spoken plane—; in his work every rhetorical figure reaches a super-rhetorical register per se. The mere fact of being written raises every figure, in Góngora's work, to a poetic power squared.

If water crystal, crystal water

Structurally, this squared metaphor may look like a reversion to simple metaphor. Dámaso Alonso has pointed out its biunivocal nature:[1] if, for example, water is metaphorized into crystal, crystal will be returned to water. That return, that boomerang movement carries an element of *marking*, indicated by an adverbial quantity. If water has been metaphorized into crystal, crystal will appear as *softly* solid water.

Crystal, snow, gold . . .

That reactive play on the part of metaphor will lead us to a certain contamination, a geometric multiplication, a proliferation of the metaphoric substance itself. All *legible* reality coincides, accelerates, and falls into place at the point where *conceits* of the metaphorical absolute intersect. When we see the word *gold* a series of metonymies leads us through an entire sequence of golden objects. The same thing happens with *crystal* and *snow* . . .

All of the *Soledades* (*Solitudes*) amount to one grand hyperbole: the final and absolute meaning of Góngora's rhetorical figures is hyperbole itself. We might well ask if in essence the baroque is not merely an immense hyperbole in which the axes of nature (according to the meaning I previously assigned to that word) have been broken, erased.

When he is not transcribing an object of perception—when none of the multiples of *snow*, *gold*, or *crystal* achieves the total reading of reality the poet wants to convey in all its density (for which no metaphorical absolute could suffice, since they would all convert that reality into something homogeneous and monochromatic; that is, they would betray it)—, then Góngora turns to the image of discourse itself. Reality—landscape—is merely discourse: a signifying, and therefore decipherable, chain. Renaissance-style landscape with a river and a few islands. How does Góngora insert us in that totality? Through the image of discourse: the islands are like *parentheses* (leafy parentheses) in the *period* of the current. This is also how line 194 of "Soledad primera" ("First Solitude") should be interpreted: *if for them a lot a little map unfolds*, in which Góngora turns to a graphic syntagma.

The Negation of Terror

If the pure level of language is that which contains no rhetorical figures (its existence is debatable, of course, since what we understand by a pure level is really a chain of *naturalized* figures), it is inevitable that distance, separation be created between the pure level and metaphorical language. Sign of the literary, in Góngora's work such separation reaches the extreme. Terror (Paulhan's term for the rejection of rhetoric) disappears: the absent signified gets lost in a tangle of possible signifieds. In the classics, the distance between figure and meaning, between signifier and signified, is always limited; the baroque enlarges that break between the two poles of the sign.

Reading Reality

In all of Góngora's metaphors, the first category, the code of reading, is the symbolic: from it a reading of reality begins. Poetry is a cultural project sustained in culture, and everything that falls outside of culture takes on the connotation of reference in relation to language. Hence the resistance that for centuries has given the adjective "Gongorine" an equivocal meaning.

The code of reading, the "faithful, although concave" mirror in which the real world finds itself reflected, is a language composed of all the cultural elements of the Renaissance: reference to mythology, astronomy, literature, the fine arts, etc. This *knowing* orders and interprets on the basis of its own conceptions. Some notions must be eliminated, others must be dealt with according to rhetorically established canons. For Góngora, poetry is not invented; on the contrary, it belongs to a world that is *already* formed, a world whose laws are fixed.

Poetry that is *trope* by its very nature, that eludes (*e-ludere*) all messages. Its lines form a series of periphrases, circles that traverse reading and whose center, although elliptical, is always present. In Góngora's periphrases, the elliptical signified functions like the "pathogenic nodal point" discussed by Jacques Lacan: it is that regularly repeated theme in the longitudinal reading of discourse (repeated like a structuring absence, like whatever is eluded), that causes words to break down when they confront it. Their breakdown denotes the absent signified. The longitudinal chain of periphrasis describes an arc: a radical reading of those breakdowns permits us to decipher the absent center.

The central reference is nature invented. A cornucopia, flowers and fruits overly illuminated against a black ground: *loaded* motifs, the Italian baroque.

Mirror

A virtual line running through the poem divides its verses into two symmetrical parts that mutually oppose and duplicate each other like mirror space and real space. On both sides of that line are found unities of sound (and sense), signifier (and signified).

It would be worth studying the continued presence of this phenomenon in all Spanish art, not only in literature. *Las Meninas* would be the instance when the mirror is placed virtually off the canvas, thereby robbing the painting's physical surface—the canvas in its literal sense—of all importance and imposing its own marginal presence.[2] What is interesting about the "First Solitude" is that this same line also runs through its story. Note that the old shepherd welcomes the shipwrecked youth like a son because he reminds him of his own son who drowned; at the end of the poem the shipwrecked youth, who had left dry land because of an unhappy romance, attends a wedding. The symmetry imposed here

> shipwrecked youth / drowned youth
> wedding realized / wedding thwarted

could be extended to the entire text, and perhaps to all four *Solitudes* if the author had completed his plan (the four ages of man: youth, adolescence, adulthood, senility; or perhaps the four places of solitude: countrysides, shores, jungles, wasteland).

The Throb of Meaning

> "may doors open externals
> on discourse, discourse on truths" [3]

Discourse is an intermediary on which "externals" open and which in turn opens on "truths." A dual motion that establishes the throb of meaning across the line of discourse (a *discrete* or, in other words, an uninterrupted line). It is this oscillation of signs, this double breach that creates the break within discourse which permits us to "read" the *Solitudes*.

The poem as perpetual change, as an always unstable substitution and an always precarious birth of signs at the site of that throbbing between the external and the truth: on the oscillating frontier of the page.

DISPERSION

False Notes / Homage to Lezama

In memoriam, to Rolando Escardó, who in 1949 gave me a copy of Orígenes,[†]

People who correct the mistakes the Cordoban liked to make about animals, believing that he took them from Pliny the Elder, separate those mistakes—such as referring to the scales on seals—from their urgent poetic necessity, forgetting all the while that he needed those scales for their reflections and their submerged metalic gliding.

José Lezama Lima, "Sierpe de Don Luis de Góngora"

A Memory

We were leaving the theater. Throughout the evening the young soloists from the Bolshoi had renewed our sense of wonder with their skill; now the stage was an empty, white box: memory brought back their flights, their bodies, tracing swift signs in the air—their writing.

In the hot, crowded vestibule, Lezama was roaring, at the center of his followers: snowy drill; Creole aristocracy flaunting Spanish dignity. A horseman right from a Colonial print, from some *Vista de Habana* ("View of Havana") by Landaluce or Hill—in the background a Plaza de Armas on the night of an open-air concert, a tree-lined boulevard crowded with buggies; angels among the battlements of Morro castle, plateresque façades. He flourished a cigar; bluish spirals unfolded, enveloping his slow gestures, his measured presence, his words.

[†]*Orígenes* (Origins) was a literary magazine edited between 1944 and 1956 by Cuban poet, novelist, and essayist José Lezama Lima, whose novel *Paradiso* was published in Havana in 1966 and translated into English by Gregory Rabassa (*Paradiso* [1974. Austin, TX: U of Texas P, 1988]). *Translator's note.*

I broke through the circular palisade of smoke to greet him.

"What did you think?" I asked him quickly.

"Look, young man," and he imposed his weighty, sententious voice, inhaling a mouthful of air, panting as if he were about to suffocate, "in the demanding Swan variations, Irma Durujanova achieved the category and majesty of Russia's Catherine the Great as she paraded on her sorrel along the frozen banks of the Volga . . . ," and he took another breath.

Lezama never saw the Volga, not to mention frozen; his comparison with the empress, which added the magnitude of the tzarist panoply to his own obesity, was more than questionable, and yet . . . no better analogy, no more textual, more appropriate equivalent of the dance than that phrase. The phrase itself, and not its integral content, its semantic substance. It was the form, the actual *phoné,* accentuated by Lezama's manner of speaking—long, open vowels, arrhythmic breathing, breaks of low Albanbergian—that in his language established neither a description nor even a "profound perception," but a vocal analogy, a phonetic dance.

The fact is that in Lezama the seizing of reality, the voracious capture of the image, works by *duplication*, by *mirage*. A virtual double that will gradually beseige and surround the original, undermining it with imitation, with parody, until it is supplanted. Now, after Lezama's definition, his enunciation, and in the unique and reversible time that is poetry, the Bolshoi dancers had *illustrated* the phrase already pronounced, they had confirmed—as examples, instances—a category.

Lezama's *démarche*, then, is metaphoric. But metaphor, the devouring *double* of reality, the displacer of *origin*, is always and exclusively of a cultural nature. As in Góngora, here it is culture that reads nature—reality—and not the reverse; it is knowledge that codifies and structures the disproportionate sequence of events. With its materials, the linguistic assembles an armature, a reflected geometry, that defines and replaces the nonlinguistic.

The cultural accuracy of those metaphors matters little: what they set in motion are relations, not contents. In the case of the dancers, the important thing was to create a dialogue between the semes /*Majesty*/ and /*Russia*/; to get the mirage working between them. The chain could have been assembled differently, with other characters, whether or not they were historically "accurate.'' To speak of Lezama's mistakes—even for the purpose of saying they do not matter—is *already* not to have read him. If his history, his archeology, his esthetics are delirious, if his Latin is ridiculous, if his French resembles the nightmare of a Marseillaise printer, and if dictionaries are useless for understanding his German, it is because what counts on Lezama's pages is not the veracity of words—in the sense of identity with something nonverbal—but their *dialogic presence*, their mirage. What counts is the texture, *French*, *Latin*, *culture*, the chromatic value, the stratum they signify in the vertical cross-section of his writing, in its display of parallel wisdom.

Dubbing

Freed from the ballast of verism, from any practice of realism—I include its worst variant: magical realism—and abandoned to the demon of analogy, Lezama's metaphors attain a remoteness from their terms, a hyperbolic freedom that in Spanish—I am disregarding other languages: the very essence of ours is baroque—is achieved only by Góngora. Here the distance between signifier and signified, the break that opens between the faces of metaphor, the breadth of LIKE—of language, since language implies that LIKE is all its *figures*—is maximum:

''Doctor Copek *like* a crow holding a moist raspberry in its beak.''

''His whole being *resembled* the relief on an Etruscan liver about to be read as an oracle.''

''The somber guitarist reacted *like* a red rooster, a bonfire sprinkled with salt or a royal page stabilized beneath an early morning shower.''

''When the Colonel came upon him, he was seated in the smoking room, absorbed in the filigree of his watch, its two covers open, *like* an Egyptian cat before an ibis.''

''But the insignificant residents of Jacksonville made fun of how, in spite of his chubby and inquisitorially long-fingered hands, he bungled the octaves, and the use of the flute stop on his instrument provoked nervous squeaks, *like* cuts made in frozen quince.''

Sometimes the rhetorical breach, the centrifugal force of the *like* is such that the approximation, the relation between the terms, seems to result from a self-determination on the part of the text, an automatic writing or dubbing.

Williams Burroughs: Dubbing†

"In writing my last two novels, *Nova Express* and *The Ticket That Exploded*, I have used an extension of the 'cut up method' I call 'the fold in method.' A page of text—my own or some one else's—is folded down the middle and placed on another page. . . . The composite text is then read as a single text because of this dubbing. Dubbing gives the writer literally infinite extension of choice. For example, take a page of Rimbaud and double it over a page of Saint-John Perse—two poets who have much in common—; any number of combinations could arise from those pages, an infinite number of images."

La Quinzaine Littéraire

Fixity

"When Picasso wants something, he paints it." In other words: he sells the painting and acquires the painted object.

(French saying)

---

†In this section, in his translation into Spanish from a French version of Burrough's comments, Sarduy has added some new wrinkles to the "fold in method," which he refers to as *doblaje* or cinematic "dubbing." This translation no doubt owes to the fact that the Spanish equivalent of the verb *fold* is *doblar*, as well as to the act of replacement and insertion of voices implicit in Burroughs's work. It must also allude to the complex doubling that both gives voice to and silences in *Written on a Body*. Although the English *dubbing* does not double precisely the suggestion of *doblaje*, it carries some not inappropriate connotations of its own, especially when folded into or doubled over Burroughs's remarks as they are translated back into English from Sarduy's Spanish. Perhaps it is not solely by chance that both the homage and the violence or abuse hinted at in *doblaje* are more evident in the English (Burroughs himself explicitly linked the "fold in method" with the "cut up method"). This reduction or substitution that, simultaneously, makes possible "infinite extension" should also permit *dubbing* to double up and unfold throughout Sarduy's essays in English and to reappear with something of the same *choteo* that *doblaje* does in Spanish. *Translator's note.*

In the antipodal terms of metaphor, the tension is first felt with the second term—after the *like*. What is cultural, linguistic, deciphers what is real. Metaphor as conjuring. If the ritual formulation of the *like* is exact, if the *is equal to* works, the second term devours the object, seizes its body. I repeat, an exactness of form, not content, which a passage from Lezama's *Paradiso* illustrates perfectly, since in it formal priority is clearly so important that the issue becomes phonetics in the strict sense.

"After Uncle Luis had shown off his knowledge of cantabile, the boy wanted even more to humiliate him, to push him again to the very visible limits of his rusticity: 'If you pronounce the word *reloj* ("watch") correctly'—and he emphasized the explosive, gutteral sounds of the *j*—, 'I'll give you the one I'm using, since I plan to buy myself another.' "

When Lezama wants something, he pronounces it. He immobilizes it phonetically, traps it among vowels and consonants, dissects it, freezes it in motion—a beetle, a butterfly in the glass of a paperweight—, reconstitutes an image so precise that the object of action is changed into a blurred, fuzzy image of the construction, the double—now the original—outlined by him.

Lezama fixes.

/Octavio Paz: "Una de cal . . ."

"Lezama's *fixity* is what prevents dispersion."

(Papeles de Son Armandans)

/Octavio Paz: "La máscara y la transparencia"

(about Carlos Fuentes)

"An enormous, joyful, painful, delirious verbal substance that might call to mind the baroque style of José Lezama Lima's *Paradiso*, if it is appropriate to use the term 'baroque' in reference to two modern writers. But the dizzyness caused us by the constructions of the great Cuban poet owes to fixity: his verbal world is that of the stalactite. Fuentes's reality, on the other hand, is one of movement, is a continual explosion. Lezama's world is accumulation, petrification, an immense verbal geology; Fuentes's is an uprooting, the exodus of languages, their meetings and dispersions."

(Corriente alterna)

Writing without Limits

In *Paradiso* we find Góngora, but also Dante—surprise: Lezama writes his *Inferno*—; Joyce—although in *Ulysses* culture is analogical and in Lezama there is no verbal play in the strict sense, for when it appears, it is attenuated by *mirage*—; Proust—the clause that bifurcates and dichotomizes its subordinates to the point of inaccuracy, until the thread is lost, until recovery is sensed, breathing becomes anguish (this must be stressed)—; Gadda, in the *Pasticciaccio*; and also Cervantes, Garcilaso, Calderón, Christopher Columbus's diary, José Martí, Saint Theresa, Quevedo, Saint John of the Cross, Casal, Mallarmé, Saint-John Perse, Claudel, Valéry, Rilke, Sade, Gênet, and apparently Jules Verne as well!

Ultimately, in literary criticism it would be useful to abandon boring, diachronic sequence, and return to the original meaning of the word *text*—textile, tissue—, considering everything written and everything yet to be written as a single, unique, simultaneous text in which the discourse we initiate at birth is inserted. A text that repeats itself, quotes itself without limits, plagiarizes itself; a tapestry that unravels so as to spin other signs, a stroma that varies its motifs infinitely and whose only meaning is that intersection, that plot contrived by language. Literature without historical or linguistic borders: a system of communicating vessels. Talk about the influence of *The Castle* on *Don Quijote*, of "The Death of Narcissus" on the *Solitudes*.

/Ah! Dialectize the polemics between Mario and Emir. *Paradiso* would be, in adjectival order, a *baroque, Cuban*, _____, _____, and *homosexual* novel. Find those terms. Fill in the blanks.

/Quote Goytisolo.

/Talk about the publication of *Orígenes*.

/Copy what I said about Lezama/Carpentier.

/Add a few Lezama-like sonnets.

/Don't fall into the trap of criticism: mimetic language, repetition of the author's style—which turns into repetition of his "tics." Avoid any expressions that sound like Lezama's.

Keep preliminary notes.

Omit the image of the beetle in the paperweight from the paragraph about *fixity*.

Add fictional characters, mine or another's, to criticism. Mix genres. Have a possible reader chime in.

Superposition

Metaphor, a way of knowing, gradually invades the story with its *is equal to*, tying together a plot of comparisons, of forced similarities. As he elaborates his poetic system, Lezama awards the most important place to the *ocupatio* of the Stoics, in other words, to the total occupation of a body. If, as he contends, it is the image that occupies the poem, it is metaphor that covers the novel's "substance or territorial resistance." The poem would be a retroactive body, created by the final image reached by the chain of metaphors; the novel, the chain itself: contiguous displacements. Progressing by ramification, imbrication, in order to form the terrain that will eventually be inhabited by the image, the metaphor alluded to by Lezama adheres so closely to its origin—the linguists' metonymy—that the two seem to blend. In this way, there is a metaphorical dimension to the Lezamesque image.

/Roman Jakobson: Metaphor and Metonymy

"Metaphor is impossible when there are problems of *similarity*; metonymy, when there are problems of *contiguity*.

"Thus, in a study about the structure of dreams, the decisive issue is to determine whether the symbols and temporal sequences employed are based on contiguity (Freudian metonymic displacement and synecdocal condensation) or similarity (Freudian identification and symbolism)."

(*Essais de Linguistique Générale*)

/Lezama: Metaphor and Image

"One of the mysteries of poetry is the relation between the analogue, or the connective force of metaphor—which as it advances creates what we could call poetry's substantive territory—and the conclusion of that advance, across infinite analogies, at the site of the image, which has a powerful regressive force, capable of covering that substantiveness. . . . What I find so wonderful about the poem is its ability to create a body, a resistant substance riveted between a metaphor, *which as it advances creates infinite connections*, and a final image, which insures the survival of that substance, that *poesis*.

(*Órbita*. Conversation with Armando Álvarez Bravo.)

Metaphor, as it advances and "creates infinite connections," assembles a palisade that is the plane of the novel, but because its nature is cultural and its references extremely wide, things Cuban (the first term, before the *like*)[†] appear as something deciphered, read across all cultures: they are defined as the superposition of those things.

Cuban reality as superposition. It is not by chance that Lezama, who has reached the inscription, the veritable foundation of the island, its make-up as a *difference* of cultures, would reconstitute its space for us in such a way. Cuba is not a synthesis, a syncretic culture, but a superposition. A Cuban novel must make explicit all the strata in that superposition, must show all its "archeological" planes—they could even be separated into tales, for example, one Spanish, another African, another Chinese—and achieve Cuban reality through the meeting of those tales, through their coexistence in the book's *volume*, or as Lezama does with his accumulations, in the structural unity of each metaphor, each line.

immediate reality / Cuban protagonist	LIKE →	cultural reference / Assyrian hunter-king, Chinese emperor, Etruscan liver, etc.	=	*Cuban reality as superposition.*

[†]This is the first of several instances of *lo cubano*, an adjective (*cubano*) made noun by the addition of the neuter pronoun *lo*. Although the expression is probably rendered most literally and most frequently by *Cubanness*, I have preferred to retain *Cuban* as an adjective, to preserve its suggestion of condition, quality, or state rather than limit those suggestions to a single "thing". As Octavio Armand has insisted, *Cubanness* reduces *lo cubano* in a very unCuban way, and is not a sonorous word. Hence the use of "what's Cuban," "things Cuban," or even "Cuban reality." *Translator's note.*

In that superposition, and this also identifies it as Cuban, an element of laughter, a discrete joke, a bit of *choteo* always slips in from the impact in collage itself. Even in Cuba's first poem, *Espejo de paciencia* (Mirror of Patience) by Silvestre de Balboa (1608), the elements of our Cuban reality seem to have been superposed, with the same density as in *Paradiso*.

/Cintio Vitier: "Espejo de Paciencia"

"What is usually considered an extravagant mistake in Balboa's poem—the mixture of elements from Greek and Latin mythology with indigenous flora, fauna, instruments, and even clothing (remember the Hamadryads "in petticoats")—is to my way of thinking its most significant and dynamic element, the one that truly links it with the history of our poetry. . . . But in the very strangeness and humor provoked by the uninhibited coupling of words like *Satyrs*, *Fauns*, *Sylvans*, *Centaurs*, *Napaiae*, *Hamadryads*, and *Naiades* with *soursops*, *star apples*, *mammees*, *avocados*, phantom *siguapas*, *night-blooming cereus*, *virijí*, *jaguars*, *viajacas*, *guabinas*, *hicatees*, *ducks*, *hutias*, there is hidden (without the author's intention or awareness, just through the simple force of names) the germ of *an elemental Cuban trait*, and that is the gentle laughter used to crack ostentation, illustriousness, and transcendence in any of their closed forms."

(*Lo cubano en la poesía*)

With *Paradiso* the tradition of the *collage* attains precision, becomes fixed and defined as "an elemental Cuban trait." Multiple sediments, which suggest the most diverse kinds of knowledge, various subject matters outcrop and confront their textures, their seams as after a quake. The limits of the disparity, the variegation of the Greco-Roman and Creole pastiche are pushed in the novel until all things strange, all the externals are recovered. Cuban reality appears then, in the violence of that encounter of surfaces—addition and surprise as heterogeneous phenomena are juxtaposed.

That confrontation and that surprise imply, in their very mechanism, a sneaky humor: the "gentle laughter" always provoked by the fortuitous. "A *seal*, on an *Ottoman* table, that touches up its

Pythagorean androgyne's nose, the *Swedish* balls, the caps of the man who robbed the *mosque*."
(*Paradiso*)

/Lezama: Things Cuban

"The fortuitous," says Lezama, "takes root in the totality of 'things Cuban,'" and he cites, as a very Cuban example, those verses by Casal: "I sense, submerged in mortal calm/ vague pains in my muscles." "That!" he asserts, "is very Cuban because of the rush it offers, its *surprise or flash*. There is a delicate way of stepping into a half-open sky, which recalls that slightly built Saint Barbara who carries in her hand a powerful sword she can barely grasp, although she uses it to behead the lightening bolt."

(Interview with Loló de la Torriente, *Bohemia*)

The Third Solitude

"There has been much discussion of the baroque in Alejo Carpentier's writing. In truth, the only *baroque* (with the entire burden that term carries, in other words the tradition of culture, the tradition of Hispanism, Manuel I of Portugal, Borromini, Bernini, Góngora), the real baroque, in Cuba is Lezama. Carpentier is neogothic, which is not the same as baroque."

(From my conversation with Emir Rodríguez Monegal)

/The universe of superposition implies or coincides with that of the baroque. *Paradiso* might be a *summa* of its themes, a hyperbole, so like Góngora's work in its execution, its swerves, its humor, and its rhetorical consistency, that the novel could be read as a Cuban "Solitude" unfurled. Góngora is the absolute presence of *Paradiso*: the novel's entire discursive and highly complex mechanism is merely a parable whose—elliptical—center is Spanish *culteranismo*. At times the similarity of the tropes is almost textual; at other times we find American versions of those same tropes; at still others, as in the first chapter, it is a marginal character who, without naming Góngora, assumes Góngora's literalness: with a Creole's total lack of inhibition, "swallowing a handful of large purple grapes," Mrs. Rialta's overpolite brother recites a few verses from the "First Solitude": "whose tooth pardoned not a cluster, even on Bacchus's forehead, much less on his vine."

If Góngora is the referent of *Paradiso*—a text's only interlocutor: another text—, by creating a rotation of readings we could apply Lezama's deciphering of Góngorism to his own work: consider writing's "poetic needs and demands" its only truth; a message that contains its code, a discourse that creates its identities and reabsorbs its contradictions, an autonomous word, an enigma that is its own response. For Lezama, critical method is an emanation from the text or, rather, its reduction, the reflection of its totality that, like a Flemish painting, the text itself contains.

/Lezama: "Sierpe de Don Luis de Góngora"

"Whether Góngora is deciphered or his zenithal evidence blinding, his hyperboles beam with the joy found in poetry as a secret gloss on the seven languages of the prism of intuition. For the first time in our history, poetry has become the seven languages that intone and proclaim, forming a different, reintegrated organ. But that robust intonation within the light, into which have been kneaded both misunderstood and undeciphered words that sound to us like the simultaneous translation of various unknown languages, produces the sententious and solemn guffaw that clarifies and skirts everything, since it kneads a larger quantity of breath, of penetrating current into newly-invented meaning."

(*Analecta del reloj*)

Anticipating the most recent theories—Bakhtin's reassessment of Russian formalism, Julia Kristeva's semiology of paragrams—, in this text Lezama defines writing as a dialogic subject, as an interaction of voices, of "*languages*" as a coexistence of all the "translations" found in a single language, an "*organ*" in which different literary functions, in the form of reminiscences, paradoxes, quotations, expressions of reverence or derision (the "*sententious and solemn guffaw*") institute, "*intone and proclaim*" that *Carnival* proposed by Bakhtin: "*robust intonation within the light.*"

/The reverse of the trivialization of Góngora—the *Solitudes* superposed on the humdrum of the day-to-day conversation—is the Gongorization of the trivial. Both processes interchange their meanings, their arrows: a conceptual ebb and flow that is another aspect of *dialogue*. In counterpoint to the quotation used by Rialta's brother to praise the grapes, here is Gongoresque rhetoric when it works with something that would seem to be unlikely material for such treatment: "One of the oarsmen, feeling indiscrete pangs from a midnight chocolate, got up to uncoil his intestinal snake."

The Inca Garcilaso

In an essay about Góngora, and in order to explain the *fascination* that Incan jewels held for him, Lezama imagines a meeting between the poet from Córdoba and the Inca Garcilaso de la Vega, "a conjecture with real basis in the world of poetry," one that starts from a historical certainty: the Inca's presence in Córdoba. Some years later, without knowing that text, Michel Butor arrived at the same conjecture.

/Michel Butor: Córdoba

"Góngora surely knew and read the Inca Garcilaso de la Vega, and that acquaintance, that meeting allow us to give this verse about the Guadalquiver—'*of noble although not of golden sands*' (which at first glance may seem like filler)—its true resonance. The word *golden* must be taken in its most literal sense. Then, from this allusion to *El Dorado* and those fabulous American rivers—which, according to public rumor, were filled with huge nuggets of gold—it will be clear that the poet is comparing Córdoba with and declaring it equal to the ancient cities of the new world such as Cuzco, 'that other Rome in his empire,' to use the words of the old mestizo priest who came from them."

(*Les Lettres Nouvelles*)

I do not know if these two proposals—Lezama's and Butor's—have a common source, which is most probable, or if it is a question of coincidence. What is curious and significant about both writers is the argument each advances. For Lezama, who bases his poetic system on the image, the meeting between Góngora and the bastard son of a European conquistador and a princess from

Cuzco is verified by a fascination, in other words, by the power of an image. For Butor—the *nouveau roman* considered itself denotative writing, a break with the *like*—it is verified by a literal reference, in other words, a negation of metaphor, of the imaginary dimension.

Archimboldo

/*Cintier Vitier: The Poetry of Lezama Lima*

"The joyous, flavorful, or furious baroque style of that popular American impulse he has studied so well increasingly shapes his language; and in these *Venturas criollas* (The Fortune of Creoles), now distanced from the affectionate jesting of his early Gongorism, more alone with Quevedo's unwieldy goblins, he applies all he has learned to his tender shyness and searing Cuban indifference."

(*Lo cubano en la poesía)*

Of all baroque themes, there is none better than food—"loaded" still lifes—for converting frozen, European forms to the proliferation of the open, gnostic space of American reality, which "knows because of the very spaciousness of the landscape itself, because of superabundant blessings"; no theme better abandons its humanistic heritage in order to become "showy texture," extravagance. Lezama's table equals the wedding banquet of Góngora "at his finest," and surpasses it with the outrageousness of Lezama's own inventions (guinea hen or hen painted with honey from the blue flowers of Pinar del Río, produced by bees from a Greek epigram; breast of guinea hen Virginia style; a double buzzing).

Creole style, however, is neither culinary motley nor the inconsistent improvisation of dishes—"affectation"—but a knowledge of precise, fixed rules:

"She turned to the pot of gumbo and said to Juan Izquierdo, 'How could you be so foolish as to put both Chinese shrimp and fresh shrimp in this dish?' Hiccoughing and pulling on his nose as if it were a slide trombone, Izquierdo answered her, 'Madame, the Chinese shrimp are used to give the soup a heartier flavor, whereas the fresh ones are like the slices of plantain and chicken thighs that some people put in gumbo to make it taste like an exotic spicy stew.' 'So much affectation,' Mrs. Rialta said, 'is not appropriate for certain Creole dishes.'''

Lezama's feast equals Flaubert's in its ostentatious presentation of trays, its tropical abundance of fruits, its rapid succession of sweets; but for illustrations of Lezama's lavish spread, of his burnished cornucopia, it would be best to look not in literature but in those painted, anthropomorphized banquets—imbrication, *collage*—created in Archimboldo's "portraits."

"He worked silently, gathering delicacies of preserves and almonds, Salamancan hams, fruits in season, Viennese pastries, liqueurs pulled from the ruins of Pompey, which had by now turned into syrup, or wine aged so long that pouring one drop on a handkerchief made it assume the characteristics of the handkerchief Mario had used to wipe his perspiration in the ruins of Carthage. Candies that left hazelnuts like panes of glass, translucent when held to the light; pineapples with sparkling facets reduced to the size of an index finger; coconuts from Brazil, reduced until they resembled grains of rice, which flaunted their bushy heads again when dipped in orchid wine."

Gadda

/Trace a parallel between Lezama and Gadda.

There are more than enough points of contact; I am going to stick to the least apparent: the *stifled* rhythms of the phrase, the anarchic distribution of punctuation, as if commas, those respiratory pauses, suddenly became imperative. In those periods, enveloping but split—broken spirals—there is something that might well be explained as an unexpected lack of air, a pneumatic problem. We must remember the evident: the pneuma, our air or breath, which in a rhetorical context designates a sustained period composed of a mounting series of prepositions, was, for Plato, the Spirit.

In the baroque masters Lezama and Gadda, in those doubles of the urban, linguistic pastiche found in Havana and Rome, *Paradiso* and *Quer Pasticciaccio brutto de la Via Merulana*, the eloquence of the vegetable kingdom, of Cuban scrolls or Flavian twists becomes a mechanical joining, a deformed nexus; multiplied adjectives and complex syntax become rhetorical counterfeit; the melodious merriment of rococo becomes squeaking, Myth becomes Satire, History becomes Farce.

/Read the preface to *L'affreux pastis de la rue des Merles* by François Wahl, substituting *Romans* for *habaneros*, Gadda for Lezama, etc.

/François Wahl: Gadda

"Romans, Gadda among them, like to sit in the Plaza Navona at night and enjoy an ice cream. A coincidence of styles here merits further study. In Bernini's rhetorical display—the Four Continents convened in a modest fountain—you find all of Cicero's amplitude, but also a somewhat exaggerated emphasis: an excess of lasciviousness in the postures, too many contrasts between the masses on the relief, which incline his art toward the 'macaronic.' Around the plaza, erect the world of inns so pleasing to all picaresque literature; but don't forget that here, in this setting of narrow churches and small baroque palaces, you find yourself in a place whose measure is exactly that of man, a place where his hopes, frustrations, and passions, both large and small, echo naturally. . . . The *Pastis* is like a concretion: surprising swerves of sediment, a slow accumulation of diverse calcification follows the water's oozing; colors have not been applied to stone, but have arisen from its depths: they are matter itself. Gadda is one of those prodigal cultural products that become veritable natural phenomena."

(From the French edition of the *Pasticciaccio*)

Written in Cuban

/"Perhaps there have already been two answers, on the level of writing, to the question of Cuban essence: the word "Cuban" has reached a pinnacle on two occasions. The first is in Martí's *Diary*, in those final pages when Martí has returned to Cuba, practically on the eve of his death, near Dos Ríos, knowing full well that he is about to die. Those pages have an almost hallucinatory

quality. From the point of view of Cuban speech they are central: there is something in them, a total upheaval; Cuban essence is expressed. Martí wrote that something which cannot be described. You have to read the page. At that moment, Martí surpassed the level of meaning, the verb *to say*; Martí *was*, he was that something, he was Cuban reality. That threshold is the ideal goal of Lezama Lima's work, in particular a recent poem titled "El coche musical" (The Musical Carriage), which is part of his book *Dador*. In "El coche musical" there is an evocation of colonial Havana, which is in the process of becoming republican, of its fairs, and of Cuban music. Note that the music is very important, because only on this level has the synthesis been fully realized."
(From my conversation with Emir Rodríguez Monegal in *Mundo Nuevo*)

In a conversation, Juan Goytisolo pointed out to me the importance of diminutives in Cuban language. How curious, he said, that a country which always creates for itself such a tremendous image of its wars would name one of its own wars the *Guerra Chiquita* (Little War). Goytisolo also stressed the caricaturing graphicness of the expression "se le cayó el altarito" (his little altar collapsed), a popular allegory for a change of luck.[†]

The *Quijote* defines and fixes a syntax; *Paradiso* a way of speaking. A Cuban *parlé* in which the diminutive or, rather, the alternation of diminutive/augumentative outlines the primary system of a game of verbal deformation. Not by chance, Lezama himself has noted that this phenomenon, which he observed in Gaucho poetry, is characteristic of American expression: one find is an augmentative, *fandangazo* (a huge fandango), that occasions further expansion because of its link to a diminutive and the humorous contraction it occasions, "hizo sonar cueritos" (he made their little hides ring). It would be possible to plot, as on a graph, the curves of desinence on each of Lezama's pages, the nearly always humorous rhythm of contractions and dilations, whose antecedents are found in the poems of *Venturas Criollas*.

[†]In other words, he fell off his pedestal. What is suggested, of course, is that on his own he was nothing to start with (good fortune lasted only as long as he was "elevated" by his little altar). *Translator's note.*

Salen el chato calaverón, la escoba alada y la planicie del manteo.

(Enter the big flat-nosed skull, the winged broom, and the plain of the cloak.)

Le buscaron balas y tapones,
pequeño tapándose las sienes:
el bobito, frente de sarampión, mamita linda.

(They brought him bullets and wads,
the small boy covering his wadded brow:
little dummy, measly forehead, lovely mommy.)

From Cuban popular speech Lezama takes the formal distortion of the disinences and also the conceptual distortion of proper names; nicknaming is the country's most deepseated and treacherous custom. With sly accuracy, Cubans systematically nickname everything that refers to them; they use nicknames to smash every attempt at solemnity and grandiloquence, employing those overgrown appellations to break up any spectacle, make fun of magnificence, throw reality to the *choteo*.

Nicknames irrupt in Lezama's discourse in this same way: elements of rupture and imbalance that return the bookish context where they occur to its role as prop, flimsy screen, or cardboard scenery from an outdoor carnival.

"*Baby Frog Face, the Governor, Segismundo the cowboy*
got their goat behinds shaking in the little dance,
their twisted keyrings chewed by dogs."

Popular wit manifested in caricature; nickname darts "in line with similarities and obvious preferences":

"They called him *The Flautist* or *The Nun* since the imagination of that neighborhood bestowed nicknames in line with similarities and obvious preferences. His blond buddies, more sighfully subtle, called him *The Tibetan Daisy*, because he wove his Philistine desire to rub elbows with writers and artists into a show of goodness."

Word plays reminiscent of argot, the shrewdness of Havana slang, also originate in popular language, and they convey its quick phrasing, its graffiti-like quality:

"The chauffeur had observed the captain's attentions toward Alberto, and he felt obliged to get *la sin hueso* (that boneless thing) wagging with the most trivial family stories, to make the usual sentimental gesture of bringing out his wallet with the picture of his wife and three kids."

Scientific argot is also present, openly jocular in its terminological precision, in the immobility of its philology; its dialogic energy is perhaps the greatest in the novel, since—as in Sade—the separation, the difference between jargon—religious in Sade, medical in Lezama—and the object it designates—an orgy in Sade, Farraluque's Pompeian member in Lezama—is so buttressed that the opening, the *décalage* becomes laughable.

In *Juliette* the narrator comments on "the extreme veneration with which the Mother Superior's orders were received," a Jesuitical paraphrase that reminds the reader of the rigorous organization of each night's erotic theater. In *Paradiso*, Saint Ignatius's vocabulary delegates its austerity to an anatomical terminology worthy of Testut:

"As the large spur of the leptosomatic macrogenitosoma entered her, she seemed about to turn over again, but its oscillations did not break through the boundaries of her sleep."

Behind Discourse

/Other idiomatic plays on words become quite apparent if we practice what could be called *lacunar reading* and consider the lezamesque sequence an orbit traced around a repressed *idiom*, a stock phrase cut out mechanically within language, which does not rise to manifest discourse, to the textual surface. This mechanism recalls Raymond Roussel's in some of his books: a process of synonymization proves to be enclosed in another, and that one in yet another. A "census" of these *emboîtements* should be taken in *Paradiso*:

"Gulping, the loud-mouth disappeared so far beneath the surface that there was nothing left of his face, and his feet, stretched out beneath an endless refraction, came to rest on banks of sand."

In this sentence, the latent word play is a very graphic expression from Cuban—and perhaps Spanish American—language: *Se lo tragó la tierra* (the earth swallowed him up).

But in another passage, the mechanism of that *latent idiom* is much more precise:

"In that village they still remember the day you and King Lulo drew out *el mal de muerte* (the evil disease) that had suddenly overcome a calf *admired by one of those people whose compliments are 'faux pas.'* "

This paraphrastic curve hides *el mal de ojo* (the evil eye, a popular Cuban expression that, according to popular superstition, refers to a curse provoked by the praise of an unwitting evildoer, "one of those people whose compliments are 'faux pas.' "

Finally, the presence of speech, which cannot be demonstrated because it must be heard—like the "*¡Pero, che!*" (But, *che!*) to which Borges refers in "La trama" ("The Plot")—is found in Lezama's exactness of impression, the swiftness of his portraits: "Marty was so Pre-Raphaelite, so lady-like, that even his quotations seemed to wear nail polish."

The fact is that in Lezama, for the first time in Cuban history, our language has acquired its full meaning, its *maternal* gravitation. In him, language has all the creative, inaugural force of the first contact with the Mother; a dialogue that will be resumed, metaphorically, in Lezama's devotion—and this trinitarian relationship between *Mother*, *Son*, and *Language* can only occur in a Catholic space—to the Virgin, the "Deipara, bearer of God." Saving language, possessing it in its vastness and infinity, has meant, for Lezama, saving the mother, staving off her death, just as in "Tombeau pour Anatole" Mallarmé wants to resurrect his son with words.

/Armando Álvarez Bravo: Conversation with Lezama

"It was in that year, '29, when the poet's fusion with his mother began. A fusion that would crystallize, becoming total, enveloping, after a few years when the two of them were alone in the house. . . . On September 12, 1964 the poet received the worst blow of his life—his mother died. . . . Almost a year before his mother's death, Lezama had a presentiment of it, and he fell into a

state of depression that made him abandon his work, lose interest in everything, withdraw into himself: not undertake his mature work as planned. When Rosa Lima died, the poet saw disappear with her everything that until then had constituted his world and his inner drive, his secret motor. Because of this event, which was followed by physical and emotional collapse, many thought Lezama was finished. But that was not so. The strength his mother had transmitted to him through the complete identification achieved between them allowed the poet to recover and, fully aware of his loss, to decide that the time had come to bring to a close everything he had done while she was still alive, to conclude his work in such a way that it would be a tribute to their very close relationship."
(Órbita)

/Investigate, without falling into psychoanalysis, Lezama's two most important signs, which are present from the first sentence of *Paradiso*: *language*—the mother—and *breathing as anguish*.

The novel begins in a chiaroscuro reminiscent of Caravaggio when Baldovina, a substitute for the absent mother, applies brutal remedies to young José Cemí, the victim of an asthma attack whose chest was "swelling and contracting as if it were an overwhelming effort to achieve a natural rhythm."

If language *in majesty*—I underscore the Catholic connotation (the Virgin) of the term—testifies to the presence of the mother, breathing as anguish would be a signifier of the father's absence. It is when his father dies, or turns into "an immense portrait" viewed by his mother, that Lezama's asthma manifests itself as a definitive oppression. He is nine when, after that loss, "severe attacks make it necessary for him to spend long periods of time in bed, preventing him from taking part in childhood games," when the two coordinates of his space are fixed, when, closed up in his room because of illness, "he develops a closer relationship with his mother at the same time that he begins to read."

Paradiso would be the net woven by those two biographical threads, those two master signs of Lezama's life: *language in majesty / presence of the mother* and *breathing as anguish / absence of the father*.

/Loló de la Torriente: Lezama

"Lezama has a rather dark complexion and fleshy cheeks; his eyes are the focal point of his face, which in his smile—and in well-timed outbursts of laughter—conjures irony and satire as the subtle link between thought and expression."
(*Bohemia*)

/Mario Vargas Llosa: Lezama

"A very cordial man, prodigiously cultured, a fascinating conversationalist when his voice is not being guillotined by asthma, enormous, and pleasant. It's hard to believe that this great expert on world literature and history, who speaks with the same picaresque familiarity about the desserts of Brittany, feminine Victorian fashions, and Viennese architecture, has left Cuba only twice in his life, both times for very short periods: once to Mexico and once to Jamaica. ("Para llegar a Montego Bay" ["In Order to Reach Montego Bay"], one of his most beautiful poems, recounts this second experience as a mythic feat, no less supernatural and magnificent than Ulysses's return to Ithaca.)"
(*Siempre*)

After "DISPERSION"

HELP (*shaking her flaming orange locks, the incandescent, vinyl blades of a windmill*): "Darling, I've discovered that Lezama is one of the greatest writers."

MERCY (*pale, frowning, like marble*): "In Havana?"

HELP (*totally diachronic*): "No, dear, in HISTORY!"

/The (increasingly hypothetical) reader of these pages: "It seems to me that all this subtle framework, so structuralist and so fashionable, besides being unpublishable gibberish, which by dint of frequent repetition has become more a question of Hispanisms than Gallicisms, remains what I'd call external, deep as *skin*. Hobbling along on pet words and expressions, the author speaks

only of *form*. But will you please tell me what's happened to the human content? Or even more importantly, what about Lezama's insular metaphysics, his Theology—he doesn't say even a word about that—his Tellurism, his Transcendence? Come on, man! Such frivolity! Such decadence!"

/*A "Progressive" Critic:* "The Franco-Cuban writer Severo Sarduy, trapped in the filigree of his Byzantine thought, freed from historical development and converted, so to speak, into a literary entelechy, is the victim of the cold abstractions of his ivory tower, since in his prodigious sleight of hand he barely alludes to reality. If there is anything to be found in *Paradiso*, it is a fierce denunciation of the corruptness of consumer society, a harsh criticism of the system of supply and demand. How long will Sarduy continue to pursue these syntheses and metaphors? Come on, man! Such frivolity! Such decadence!"

/*The Chorus*: "Such frivolity! Such decadence! Such frivolity! Etc. . . ."

EROTICISM

/Cintio Vitier: Lezama

"He is the only one of us who can organize discourse like a medieval chase. The only one capable of unknitting the brow of Don Luis de Góngora."

(*Lo cubano en la poesía*)

I conclude by addressing the theme of eroticism in order to accord it greater importance, but through displacement. Where I sense erotic energy in *Paradiso* is not only in the overly famous chapter about possessions nor in the explicitly sexual passages but also in the book's entire body, throughout the entire margin between quotation marks that it opens in the wider band of Cuban language, precisely because of having been comprehended in that band, because of synthesizing it in the mirror, *faithful although concave*, where it is reduced. What supports the erotic function of *Paradiso* is language itself, the sentence itself with its slowness, with its intricacy, with its proliferation of adjectives, of parentheses inside other parentheses, of subordinate clauses that in turn branch out, with the hyperbole of its *figures* and the way it progresses by accumulating fixed structures, pleasure based on its own *orality*.

/Roland Barthes: Pleasure and Language

"Aside from incidents of transitive or moral communication (*Pass me the cheese* or *We sincerely want peace in Vietnam*) there is in language a pleasure of the same nature, the same quality as erotic pleasure, and that pleasure in language is its truth."

(*La Face Baroque)*

From the very first sentence until it finally opens toward the *Purgatory* which will one day conclude the *Cuban Comedy*, *Paradiso* is that truth. If Lezama's self-reflecting word can attain the height of baroque abundance, the helicoidal displacement of Borromini's cupolas, the endless proliferation of the Churrigueresque, the minting of cultures that occurred during the reign of Manuel I of Portugal, and the vegetal writhing of art nouveau, it is precisely because his word has been freed of all transitive ballast, of that *about* (in the Joycean sense: I do not write *about* something, I write something) which is the injury inflicted by information, by its morality, and has thus been restored to its fundamental eroticism, to its truth.

I have referred to Góngora's faithful although concave mirror because in *Paradiso* that eroticism passes through the reflection or the reduction of the Image. The image, which in Lezama is not transitive and whose only function is to "imagine."

If the discovery and the expression occasioned by the image cause enjoyment, it is because such is the feast of verisimilitude: the rescue of realities that were lost, among infinite possible realities, when History selected its reality. The image illuminates historical uniqueness—because Western time is linear and single—with the potential multiplicity of its realities. The poet's role is to discover those potentialities, make them visible, reflect them in the concavity of language and even use them to displace the *truth* of written History. His voluptuousness, his delight consists in stopping time in the instant when all the *alea* reduce to one, of shuffling lost images—the mediators between poetry and history—and decreeing their truth. Writing is seizing the *possible* and its exclusions.

Lezama's image is endowed with an ascendent force, a teleological arrow that seeks its goals in its textualization: writing codifies that nascent state "in endless evaporation," that certainty of the absurd found in discarded images, flip sides, blank cards, in the waltzing of facts around their own importance.

"False" stories—Julius Caesar courting the lares of the Praetor like a transvestite layered with make-up—, or ghost stories—Hernando de Soto in America adapting *La Quête du Graal*: he sought a flying cup that held the water of eternity—, or the hallucinatory, magic reliefs of textual history—the branch of fire that Columbus saw falling over the sea; the large dog chewing on a wooden column containing signs and advancing among the Indians—are the paragrams, the underlying readings of time's linear and explicit discourse.

History's cycle is the displacement, the rotation among men—texts—that discover or engender those images and others that carry them out.

It was Martí who, in visible reality, in the band of Facts, exposed Cuba's first imaginary roots, roots that were best defined in his own *Diary*. Lezama discovered another of our Images, which some day, someone, will make visible.

Homage to Lezama

I

The buck, against the orange
of the forest, passes, wet,
swift. The curdled air
adds to the forest a band

of scattered hoops. In those
cartilages of landscape
he separates, in the surf
or in the garden of his bones.

II

The frozen river, its margins covered with tapestries of obscure, dense signs, the open sea returning the voices and apples that float along the shore, nearer, farther, always writing the same texts on the sand, there where the water was about to erase, had already erased the textures, where the frozen river emptied, the margins of tiny white stones covered with purple tapestries, the open sea returning the voices, the apples that float along the shore, nearer, farther, always writing the same texts on the sand, the Book of Books, the description of a face, there where the water was about to erase, had already erased the textures.

Later the final thaws merge and roll carrying along green stones and birds, at night their murmur shakes the mountain until the frozen river empties, the margins covered with tapestries of obscure, dense signs, the open sea returning the voices and apples that float along the shore, nearer, farther, always writing the same texts on the sand there where the water will erase the textures that are barely visible on the quavering edge, on the purple plain, separated at times by spots of saltpeter, by the body of a fish, by the frozen line of the river mouth stretched between margins covered with tapestries of obscure, dense signs, far from the open sea, returning the voices, the apples that float along the shore, nearer, farther, that always write the same texts on the sand, there where the water will erase the textures, will form the delta of a frozen river, its margins covered with obscure, dense signs, the open sea returning the voices, the golden apples, points of flexible triangles, shadows on the rocky bottom, caught between blocks of ice in the river, between the black lines of the margins covered with obscure, dense signs and the open sea.

III

Pages covered with gold letters. As the Reader progresses, light sifted through the date palms reflects signs onto the wall, an instant on the black sand.

At each movement of his hand, at each new page, writing appears on the edges, between the red stones, again on the wall, along the wall where the map of the previous page has just been erased, the signs falling toward the sand, stars.

IV

Those kites, with the big fringed one from Las Marías
humming like crazy and grazing the moon.
Of the dance, Marquesano, and the conga no trace
of shutters nor invitation to open and peer out.
They drank beer in their bugles
and the dancer of Macorina was there.
China Dolly hasn't come nor Piñata
Eyes. Skin Flute, he brought it on himself.
We are here to stay.

V

Day is blinding,
Night a purple dampness.
The hanged men
spin like tops
—eyes open,
faces caked with make-up—.
They are not guitars.
Don't be shocked when you see
the scorpion cutting cane.

/Paris, XII.67

Dear Mr. Lezama:

The enclosed notes summarize a better-organized and more extensive piece I have begun about your work. I have systematically employed collage—poems, the superposition of other texts—, an oblique approach, and parody, hoping to create, in the image of *Paradiso*, a plurality of voices, and to provoke with their meeting the "gentle Cuban laughter" that breaks up a monochordous tone.

Be kind with your criticism.

I have received only the first pages of your novel in French; I regret that etc.

PRIMARY STRUCTURES

TOWARD AN URBAN ART

I

Because the word *city*, in its semantic imprecision, encompasses notions that become very diverse—, from more or less rural agglomerations to the megalopolis—it might seem that a radical severance took place when the baroque city was established. At the time the urban complex was decentralized, a break occurred with respect to spatial coordinates, which until then had been "logical"—a break analogous to the one that during the same period decentralized the space of language with its rhetorical mutations—and, in the ways of urban life, the *crisis of intelligibility* began.

Devoid of its natural points of reference, of a right-angled topology that mapped out its linearity on or in relation to rivers, walls or ruins, ramps, and moats, which spread out from the town square or the cathedral—even then the *cathedra* commanded priority—open, like poetry, to a space that was increasingly metaphorical, increasingly skeptical of the innocence of "natural" language, the city would now try to imagine itself a human *place*. It would try to establish well-ordered paths within its body, would try, in spite of everything, to be *legible*. We are still living in that search for a *legible urbanization*, in the space of rupture hypertrophied by the Industrial Revolution.

It is no accident if Góngora is the one who best defines this demand for reading: "if for them a lot a little map unfolds." The chart or map as a method of deciphering, but, above all, the reductive violence of its surface (*if a lot/a little*). This urgency to create a reductive, readable parallel code of access and orientation in a space that no longer contains any index, in an expanse without landmarks where possible routes are concealed like enigmas, is still the basis of urban practices.

The house is the place of the Self; the city, the place of the Other. Sphere of the erotic search: a body waits for us, but the road leading toward it—our *word*—is almost impossible to formulate in the excessive codification of urban *language*. A road that is invaded, erased at the very moment it is roughed out, a blind sign in the empty, uninterrupted repetition of the streets.

To create new indices, imagine surfaces that provide direction, totally artificial markers: faced with the city, this is our attitude, this explains our *vertigo of signposting*.

Only visual perceptions count, then. Texts, lights, arrows, clues, posters that arise as authoritative, iconic presences: fetishes—these are our structural indices. All other perceptions—auditory, olfactory, etc.—disappear in today's city, whose sole mechanism is one of speed, mechanization.

In Rome, the sound of fountains can guide us through the maze of narrow streets; in Havana, the smell of the ocean; in Istanbul, the voices of muezzins, but only arrows and *hypergraphic* panels will guide us through the cloverleaf of highways superposed on Stockholm, or along the identical avenues of suburban Paris. Schematic, collective elements that structure our image of the city. To them we owe our sense of urban totality. They mark our route toward the Other.

II

On the symbolic plane, until now the city has been explored only as a theme. Its representation may or may not be realistic, but when our gaze intersects the ribbon of city in the *View of Delft*, it reconstructs the right-angled topology mentioned earlier, just as it does when intersecting the foreground of an empty space by de Chirico. This art bases its practice on a sense of "Nature" that is now worn out, on an epistemology of the *center*. Cities that are "realistic" (Vermeer), oneiric (Klee, Wols), metaphysical (de Chirico), flat (Portocarrero), scattered (Dubuffet): what the artist tries to give us, what he seeks to make the object of our gaze, our optical conventions, is always an *illusion of space*.

True urban painting would be painting that did not try to deceive us; on the contrary, canvases would make their methods, their artifice explicit, and these would appear—like the city of today—as pure groupings of signals, conventions, codes.

That literalness, which might be called "graphic," could be signified as follows. I venture three possibilities:

a) geometry whose only content would be its own factitiousness; lines that would eliminate any tricks—illusions of perspective, depth, successive planes, etc. To confront us with the surface of a painting, to denounce geometry as just one more conventional system: this direction can be sensed in Malevich's efforts (*White on White*), Rodchenko's suprematism or non-objectivism, Tatlin's works. Albers's entire production, whose importance we have scarcely begun to glimpse, becomes perfectly clear within this optics.

b) painting as *parodic signposting* that would present itself as the mockery of the very act of signing. All systems of urban imagination would be explored, but they would be employed in reverse, either emptied of their messages or made to look ridiculous. Some paintings by Larry Rivers and recent work by Pablo Mesejean and Delia Cancela—the "*signifying tokens*" of the employees of the Instituto Di Tella—belong to this parody.

c) painting whose principal referent would be the canvas itself. Neither matter nor textures, nor the chromatism of lyric abstraction, but the literal, *concrete support* of the canvas, which would not try to disappear in the "universe" created by the painting, but would become its theme. Newman and Rothko established that space of plastic literalness with seemingly monochromatic surfaces. Franz Kline also worked in this vein, reducing the painting to its gesture, to the speed of action, of the plastic ritual. So did Yves Klein.

This possibility has been fully realized, however, not in painting but in the sculptures of the *minimalists*. Nothing better emphasizes the *support*, nothing makes the tautological path of urban art more explicit than *primary structures*: Robert Morris's split cylinders, Sol Lewitt's serial or modular permutations, Beverly Pepper's repeated geometries, Tony Smith's monumental topologies, and, above all, that metaphor of the skyscraper, of the room, and of current urban ideology created by Larry Bell's cubes.

CUBES

One of our culture's persistent prejudices demands that the *support* be obliterated from all artistic production. In painting, that unremitting censorship has been exercised against the canvas—the presence of textile (text), of empty space—and the substance of artistic materials—pigments, powders; in literature, it has been exercised against the page and against graphicness; in sculpture, against the armature, the (geometric, hidden) skeleton that reinforces the object.

The reason for such censorship is that civilization—and above all Christian thought—has destined the body for oblivion, for *sacrifice*. Consequently, everything that refers to the body, everything that signifies it in any way, is ultimately considered a transgression.

The underlying networks of our understanding are destined to perpetuate that oblivion, that sacrifice. The canvas—considered the material support, or body, of the painting—and the armature in sculpture, are perforce concealed in order to achieve an illusion of space, an original *logos* that, not being part of the object, can organize it from a distance.

If Larry Bell's art disorients us at first this is because in an irreversible way and through its own literalness it puts an end to all prejudices about transcendence. In his production, and because of the privileged place awarded to that literalness, in other words to body, sculpture, he destroys the notion of art as a reference to something other than its own physique: the support, the armature is precisely what constitutes the work. In their denotative presence, Larry Bell's cubes simultaneously synthesize and transgress the following pairs of opposites:

armature or hidden structure / sculpture or visible form
theme / object
opaqueness / transparency

This operation produces its own space, which, like the space of Artaud's "theater of cruelty"—there is, in fact, a theatricality involved in exhibiting a group of cubes—is "closed, produced from within itself and not organized from the vantage of an absent site devoid of place, a pretext, or an invisible utopia."[1]

An eighteenth-century grammarian[2] compared language to painting by defining nouns as forms, adjectives as colors, and verbs as the canvas itself. According to this comparison, the empty canvas and its analogue, the minimal spatial unit, the *cube*, would be the primary bodies of a *verbal art*. The verb is the support of all the work's attributes; the cube, the support of all possible forms.

By showing us the original unit, the *cube*, by stressing its literalness, and by reducing art to the non-representation that is minimal representation, Larry Bell calls into question our notions about the object, about the artistic ''product,'' about the relation between the *emotional aspect* and the *conceptual aspect* of sculpture.

FREE TEXTS AND PLANE TEXTS

Let's look at a Pop painting, a Lichtenstein, for example: a blond woman is crying (her tears are enormous), and an irregular shape containing a text, the most clichéd expression of some clichéd feeling, flows from her mouth. What is it that confers on this object plastic distinction, iconic authority, the fundamental ambiguity of a work of art? It has, simultaneously, the physical presence of the redundant, of evidence, and the absolute absence of any image as reference, as the definitive loss of the object that is named, figured. Two explanations could be ventured:

1) The painting is the product of an isolation. It presents, of course, a serial story (a comic strip or a photo-novel) separated from its context, its sequence. We are in the presence of a sign ripped from the *graphic syntagma* to which it belonged.

2) With enlargement, the graphic technique has become explicit. The dots of primary colors that make up the image are so important, the reproduction so obvious, that—especially if we consider the insignificance of the "content"—it could be said that we are looking at an art "*that provides not information about reality but information about customary forms of information,*" an art "*that refers less to social content than to the structures involved in transmitting that content.*"[1]

In her first book—*El pensamiento común, textos libres* (Common Thought, Free Texts)—Basilia Papastamatíu creates a literary space by using an analogous procedure.[2] She includes units of a given verbal sequence (a description, a declaration of love, an interior monologue), but they are separated from their context, cut into sections. The articulation of these units or *syntagmatic nuclei* produces texts whose mystery (like that of Lichtenstein's paintings) could be defined as precisely their total presence, their absolute being-there, with no referent except the page itself.

(The novels of Ivy Compton-Burnett were an early exploration of discourse. Nathalie Sarraute advanced contemporary art by decreasing to the point of banality, of ridicule, what her sequences *signified*—soothing intentions, set phrases, commonplaces—in order to emphasize the *signifying* articulation that occurred in them.)

Basilia Papastamatíu's most recent texts emphasize the parallel discussed above. In the same way that Lichtenstein moves from the enlargement of comic-strip fragments to the enlargement of objects with a strong cultural connotation (the Parthenon, a Picasso) and that Rauschenberg incorporates copies of Velásquez's *Venus* in his prophetic compositions, Basilia Papastamatíu uses a Spanish classic, Montemayor's *Diana*, as a *syntagma*. On the pastoral texts of "Spain's most florid talent," the author has superposed her own texts. This is not, however, a question of *collage* but of *bricolage*, in the sense that Lévi-Strauss has used the word.[3] It does not involve the simple superposition of materials, of *linguistic textures*, but an organizing, a structuring of those materials to form a new, liberated text in which the *syntagmatic cuts* are (practically) unnoticeable.

In 1961, the poet Nanni Balestrini took one fragment from Michihito Hachiya's *Hiroshima Diary*, another from Paul Goldwin's *The Mystery of the Elevator*, and another from the Tao Te Ching and fed them as punch cards to an IBM 7070 electric brain.[4] The result was his book, *Come si agisce, Poemi piani*.[5] Although Italian criticism, clinging to the remains of an obsolete humanism, still discusses the work's "dehumanization," "coldness," and "lack of emotion," I would not hesitate to compare the reading of the *Diana* with this book by Balestrini (which I refuse to call an "experiment"; literature is always "experimental").

That the poet, freed from all romantic residue, continues the work of machines, that beauty can be created with an *ars combinatoria* worthy of those machines, that the author's "mission" is merely to prolong the *laboro di programmazione* now seem part of the present to me.

Free Texts and Plane Texts announces a work in which the deceptive notion of "human being" has been liquidated.

FROM THE PAINTING OF OBJECTS TO OBJECTS THAT PAINT

I

As early as 1912 Kandinsky was writing that art would abandon traditional naturalistic forms and orient itself toward total abstraction or total realism. The latter, he says, "is an effort to eliminate the external artistic elements from a painting and embody its content through a simple (non-'artistic') representation of the object." He later adds that "every object (even a cigarette butt) has an inner sound independent of its external meaning. That sound grows stronger if the external meaning, the meaning of the object in everyday life, is suppressed."[1]

Total abstraction, total realism . . . Kandinsky was to explore the first of those possibilities. Contemporary painting is investigating the realm of the second, which is undefined because it is current: an art of the object, art with objects, objects as works.

The Cubist "collage" frees the object from its meaning in everyday life, but newspaper clippings and musical scores have lost their usual meaning in Picasso and Braque because they have been invested with another meaning: integrated into the syntactic whole of the painting, they function as signs of composition. Printer's type and musical staves are now materials. Not texts: textures that oppose or complement the textures of the oil: paint.

Dadaist and Cubist "collages" are diametrically opposed. Dada also separates the object from its utilitarian value. But rather than becoming integrated, that object is made the *theme* of the painting. As the relief of the canvas, the object is subject; it takes possession of plastic space and, at the same time, blasphemes that space through its emanation and ridicule.

Here it is necessary to mention a name synonymous with adventure: Marcel Duchamp. In 1916, while he was designing the glass panels of *The Bride Stripped Bare by Her Bachelors, Even,* Duchamp exhibited a rusty metal comb with an inscription, and the following year, the famous *Fountain*, that inverted urinal signed by Richard Mutt. Other *readymades* soon appeared, in Buenos Aires, in Paris, and again in New York.

Surrealism was to inherit this irreverent devotion to "things," a proliferation that would find its best definition in the dexterity of Oscar Domínguez. *Exact Sensibility* was a white globe from which a hand protruded that was plunging a hypodermic needle back into the globe. A rubber horse was passing through a toy bicycle. A figure with a head made from a ping-pong ball, completely wrapped in string, dangled one of its legs inside the case of a clock. A swan floated in a chalice.

In 1936 the object reached its apotheosis. Let it suffice to mention the exhibition in the Charles Ratton gallery. In that exhibition there were *natural objects* (agates, lumps of bismuth that looked like printing-type, carnivorous plants, a stuffed ant-bear, an enormous egg); *interpreted natural objects* (a monkey among some ferns); *incorporated natural objects* (shells in the sculptures of Max Ernst); *perturbed objects* (completely disfigured utensils found in the ruins of Saint Pierre de la Martinique after the eruption of Mount Pelé in 1902); *objects trouvés* (a book recovered from the bottom of the sea, a star-shaped biscuit signed Raymond Roussel); *interpreted objects trouvés*, *American*, and *Oceanic objects*, *readymades*, *mathematical objects*, and *surrealistic objects*. I will note two of these last examples: Miró's stuffed parrot, perched on a hollowed-out block of wood containing a doll's leg and flanked by a pendulum and a map; and, the hit of the exhibition, Meret Oppenheim's *Fur-covered Cup, Saucer, and Spoon*.[2]

This oneiric celebration marks the end of an era. Kandinsky's intention has been left far behind. Here, and without exception—if there is an exception it is the *Mobile* exhibited by Calder—the object is assimilated into *the other*, the enemy. If objects are shown, it is in their strangeness; if combined—a mechanism similar to the way dreams work with words—, it is to create a bastard, mocking entity and "because the word *object* is primarily a synonym for *resistance*. A world devoid of resistances could not contain objects."[3] The world of production is that non-esthetic space; uniformity, raw material interpreted or erased by the artist's irony.

II

In Pop Art the opposite occurs. The hot dog; the truck tire; Lichtenstein's glass atomizer; Claes Oldenburg's chocolate cake, sausages, and slices of meat; Rauschenberg's Kennedy—which only in this sense do I consider Pop—; Martial Rayesse's pear; the now too-familiar oversized Coke bottles and comic strips—in none of them is there the slightest intention of irreverence.[4] Here is a reconciliation, a respect, almost a glorification of the world of "things." If this Brave New World produces horrors, Lichtenstein makes them bearable for us, we are told by Robert Rosenblum. The artist himself says: "We like to think of industrialization as being despicable. I don't really know what to make of it. There's something terribly brittle about it. I suppose I would still prefer to sit under a tree with a picnic basket rather than under a gas pump, but signs and comic strips are interesting. There are certain things that are useful, forceful, and vital about commercial art. We're using those things."[5]

Duchamp declared that "Dada had nothing to do with the fine arts in the strict sense . . . it was negation, total rejection."[6] According to Rauschenberg, "Dada was *against*, I'm *for*," and about a *readymade* he says: "It was a bicycle wheel placed on a chair. I found it more beautiful than all the paintings in the exhibition."

The same determination to employ things (and not their images) is found in the New Realism group of the Paris School, but their reverence for the object is doubtful. In the "accumulations" of Arman and Deschamps, in the leftover dinner "fixed" by Spoerri, the mangled "*affiches*" by Hains, Villeglé, Rotella, Dufrène, reality, objects are present but distant, *analyzed*. Françoise Choay has compared this attitude with that of the New Novel.[7] To approach Spoerri's work—could we call it sculpture?—is to discover this critical treatment, this analysis to which the *neo-realists* subject data from their immediate perceptible surroundings. Our first impression is one of triviality, of aggressiveness to the point of dullness: there is a scale with various units of weight on one of its pans and four metal letters like those of a linotype or those used for advertisements on the other. These letters, apparently in no particular order, are M. O. T. Y. and S.

We have already turned away, leaving this object to look at another, when in our memory its double, its blurry—although immediate—recollection acquires a presence, a condition of palpability. It is present before (far from) our senses like a tactile *trace*, with all the corporeality of things *written*.

The fact is that the resonance of this object, its secret force, is inscribed and sustained on a level outside the plastic, in that domain of all expression and all relevance which is *language*.[8] This work *objectivizes* a rhetorical figure of current language, it is the materialization of a phrase. In this case—let me emphasize that I have chosen the simplest possible example—: *words must be weighed* (*il faut peser les mots*).

It might be fair to ignore this exercise because it is somewhat forced—a play on word play, stale surrealism, left-over Dada; it would be much less fair not to investigate the way it serves as a sign, the way it can be justified in the structure of a visual rhetoric.

An alternative history of painting, as visual rhetoric, would be the achievement of this age: the *antithesis* of Caravaggism, Poussin's *metonymies*, the metaphors of surrealist painting.[9]

In Spoerri's search, in many of the works in this group, if the object appears it simultaneously takes leave, its *being-there* is a referent, a state of being like language, which is to say a negation of its presence as object. With this object that appears in order to denote its absence, another era draws to a close, for in its own way this work is also an apotheosis, albeit a negative one, of the "thing."

III

Recently the literary supplement of the *London Times* devoted an issue to the avant garde, with a cover by Tinguely. The illustration shows an avalanche of objects: the steering wheel of a car from which a flagpole, holding a camel, protrudes; an old airplane; a parchutist seen from behind; a fork thrust in a duck; etc. The drawing—Tinguely's painting—differs only slightly from drawings by the Dadaists, Surrealists, Pop artists.

It is when we enter the Museum of Modern Art in Stockholm that we understand Tinguely's work (the final stage of the path of "total abstraction" foreseen by Kandinsky?) to be representative of all contemporary sculpture. In the main hall of the museum we are greeted by the artist's *Painting Machine*.

In exchange for a coin, the machine will execute a painting right before our eyes. The consumer's role is limited to choosing the colors, which he places at the end of some tongs, to stopping the curious contraption by pressing a button, and, of course, to signing the "work," which—predictably—always turns out to be gestural, *action painting*, and at times even seems to be an imitation of Joan Mitchell.

I will note only parenthetically the debatable esthetic result of the machine's efforts. What interests me is that between *paintings with objects* and this *object that paints* stretches our century's entire dialectics in the fine arts. Let's return to that page from the *Times*: one of the most surprising things is that Tinguely has signed it very hesitantly, has then signed again a few inches below, has almost completely scratched out the second signature, and finally signed a third time, adding a question mark, as if he were uncertain about his responsibility for the work.[10]

In the same way that we considered ourselves producers of language and now know that we are produced, conditioned by its structures, the object that paints refers us to our *reality*: little by little—as I have tried to show in these notes—, the object and its inner sound have been freed to such an extent that we have become their object. The painter from active to passive producing machines that paint what he thinks he paints, freeing self, *gesture*, *action*.

To add to the art of the object, to objects as art, an *art by objects* would be to rethink the "external" meaning that Kandinsky tried to suppress. Because in this evolution of total realism, the suppressed external realm has been—and I believe this is not an exaggeration—whatever the adjective *human* connotes, at least in the way we *still* use it.

This merits a revision of painting. In the light of a revision of language.

SIMULATION

I. COPY / SIMULACRUM

We dress for our own pleasure and get off on each other. It's our own small world; within it we understand and are understood and we do what we want. When we put on our clothes, we feel free. If other people want to share in our joy and freedom, they're welcome too. There's strength and self-confidence in the way I dress.

Suddenly, I don't feel ugly anymore.

Gilles Larrain, *Idols.*

The transvestite does not imitate woman. For him, *à la limite*, there is no woman; he knows—and paradoxically he may be the only one who knows this—that *she* is just appearance, that her world and the force of her fetish conceal a defect.

The transvestite's cosmetic erection; the glittery aggression of his eyelids, quivering and metallicized like wings on a voracious insect; his voice displaced, as if it belonged to another character, always off stage; the mouth drawn over his mouth; his own member, all the more present for being castrated—their only purpose is the stubborn reproduction of that ubiquitous though deceptive icon: the mother who has got it up and is dubbed by her double, albeit only for him to symbolize that the erection is just appearance.

The transvestite does not copy; he simulates, since there is no norm to invite and magnetize his transformation, to determine his metaphor: instead, it is the non-existence of the worshipped being that constitutes the space, the region, or the support of his simulation, of his methodical imposture between laughter and death.

Animal mimesis, according to Roger Caillois, "occurs in various guises, each of which has an analogous human manifestation: *transvestism*, *camouflage*, and *intimidation*. Myths of metamorphosis and the pleasures of disguise correspond to transvestism (true *mimicry*); legends about hats or cloaks of invisibility correspond to camouflage; fear of the evil eye and of the paralyzing (*médusant*) gaze and the use people make of masks, principally, but not exclusively, in so-called primitive societies, correspond to the intimidation provoked by ocelli (*ocelles*) and complemented by the appearance of the terrifying mimesis of certain insects."[1]

"The human transvestite is the imaginary apparition of mimicry's three possibilities and their convergence": *transvestism* in the strict sense, stamped on the unbounded drive of metamorphosis, of transformation cannot be reduced to the imitation of a real, set model, since it strikes out in pursuit of an infinite unreality that is accepted as such from the start of the "game" and is more and more fleeting and unattainable—to be more and more of a woman, until the line is crossed and woman is surpassed, the "folie douce" denounced by an ex-transvestite from the Carrousel;[2] but also *camouflage*, since nothing insures that the chemical—or surgical—conversion of men into women does not have as its hidden goal a kind of disappearance, invisibility, *effacement* and erasure of the male in the aggressive clan, in the brutal male horde and, to the extent that he shares their separation, difference, deficiency, or excess, in the female horde as well, a disappearance or obliteration connected to the transvestite's lethal drive and his fascination with fixity, which in its turn is also fascinating; and finally, *intimidation*, since the frequent incongruity of his make-up, the evidence of artifice, and his motley mask are paralyzing, terrifying: I recall, for example, the panic that overcame a friend, a pseudo-Valkyrie, in the cabarets of Tangiers during the '60s, where every night, opulent and oxygenated transvestites spread out over the city like phosphorescent bands of recently opened chrysalises: saffrony Andalusians with cloying, ritualistic hands, stoned Dahomeans, acromegalic Canadians smothering the difficult passages of a Dorisdaysean lip-sync. I can see the distraught face of my terrified friend when he was brushed, as if by lethal elytra, by the sharp, starched organzas of pleated skirts, the poisoned flowers clutched in skinny yellowish hands, and also the cheap, sickeningly sweet perfume bought in the Medina, which flooded the whole joint even before the dancers entered, shaking to the Swahili voice of Miriam Makeba.

Yet another radiance roves symmetrically over transvestites and insects. Man can paint, invent, or re-create colors and forms that he arranges on his exterior, the canvas outside his body, but he is incapable, impotent when it comes to modifying his own organism. Transvestites, who manage to radically transform that organism, and butterflies can paint themselves, make their bodies the support of their work, convert the emanation of color, the bewildering arabesques and incandescent inks into physical ornament, into an "autoplastic" art, although their creations, "repeated indefinitely, cannot avoid a cold, immutable perfection."

If we use Hugh B. Cott's massive study, *Adaptive Coloration in Animals*, and interpret the transvestite's cosmetic show in relation to animal chromatism,[3] his chromatic panoply will be easier to decipher. Following Cott's divisions, transvestism involves *apatetic* colors, in other words colors designed to mislead, and among them the transvestite would work from the range of *pseudaposematic* colors, those that warn in reverse. If, on the other hand, we assume that the transvestite tries to attract men, that his entire metamorphosic effort has meaning only as a snaring of the male—a highly improbable theory—the color of his make-up and his various somatic manifestations would be *anticryptic*, like those of the mantis, which changes into a leaf or a flower so its prey will approach without suspicion. When an insect takes on a form that is attractive to its prey, such as the appearance of a particular flower where the victim usually feeds, its colors are *pseudepisematic*. This term might apply to transvestites if we were to assume that they imitate women and that women are the customary receptacles of men, two questionable premises. The animal-transvestite does not seek a friendly appearance in order to attract (nor a disagreeable appearance in order to dissuade), but an embodiment of fixity in order to *disappear*.

Although I have likened human transvestism to a lethal drive from the point of view of animal *theatrics*, this drive emanates instead from camouflage, a "disappearance, an artificial loss of individuality that dissolves and ceases to be recognizable," and which presupposes "immobility and inertia" (Caillois 81 and 82).

Finally, for its part the lethal is no more than an extreme form, an excess of the squandering of one's self, and if we take into account the uselessness of animal mimesis and the fact that it represents nothing more than an unbridled desire for waste, for dangerous luxury, for chromatic magnificence, a need to display colors, arabesques, filigrees, transparencies, and textures, even if they serve no purpose—as numerous studies show—,[4] we will have to accept, as we project this desire for the *baroque* onto human conduct, that the transvestite merely confirms how "in the natural world there exists a law of pure disguise, an indisputable, clearly proven practice that consists in managing to pass for someone else, that cannot be reduced to any biological need derived from competition among the species or from natural selection" (99).

Stranger: And of all forms of play, could you think of any more skillful and amusing than imitation?

Plato, *The Sophist,* 234b

But if the beast is to be trapped, enveloped in the nets that argument has devised to snare him—Platonic dialogue proceeds by images from falconry or war, as if logic arose only in the realm of aggression, in the interval of violence—, if the Sophist is to be caught and handed over to the sovereign, it is imperative that the art of image-making be divided, "so that if he should find a hiding place in some part of this mimesis, we must follow hard upon him, relentlessly dividing any section that protects him. It must never be possible for him or any other species to boast of having eluded a persecution so methodical in both its attention to detail and its scope."[5]

The important thing is that the division of mimetic forms is patterned after a "hunt," a pursuit; through this process of partitioning it collaborates in a kind of terror: the magician, the imitator, the creator of illusions, the simulator must be surrounded. Are these "beasts" copyists? A person engaged in copying—the first form of mimicry—reproduces the model's exact proportions and colors each part appropriately. But difficulties arise when an artist tries to sculpt or paint a large-scale work: if the object's true proportions are reproduced, the upper parts look too small and the lower parts too large, since we see some at close range and others at a distance. In this situation the proportions used are those that "give the illusion" of the model. This involves a simulacrum: "It is the weakness of human nature that grants magic power to the use of perspective in painting, like the art produced by illusionists and all their ingenious inventions."[6] In which of these fields bounded by intimidation, aligned with the power of verisimilitude, should the Sophist be confined? Where to put the subversion of Platonism that would develop on an increasingly grand scale from mimicry to baroque painting? Copies-icons or simulacra-phantasms? "If the copies or icons are good images, and well formed, it is because they are endowed with likeness. But resemblance must not be understood as external relation: it exists less between two things than between a thing and an Idea, since it is the Idea that comprises the relations and component proportions of the inner essence." Simulacra, on the other hand, "work surreptitiously, stealthily, at whatever they work toward (object, quality, etc.), employing aggression, insinuation, subversion 'against the father,' without passing through the Idea."

Rather than affect the essence of the model and its precise, respectful reconstruction, the phenomena we are dealing with—especially in the case of human sexual transvestism—seem determined to produce its *effect*. Hence the intensity of their subversion—the capture of surface, skin, wrapping, without passing through the Idea, the central, founding principle—and the aggressiveness provoked in defenders of traditional values by the strangeness of their theatricality, which operates as if in a void, the fixity—an attribute of the lethal—of their stolen representation, and the challenge posed to the entire spectrum of economic ideologies by the ostentation of their pointless expenditure.

The model and the icon that imitates it, that tries to duplicate its truth, its ultimate identity, are relegated, passed over in a single listing of accuracies and fidelities: those abandoned or disdained—fascinating in the mirror of their immobility, the rapture of their visual attributes—by adepts of exhibition and play, artists who have become the support that sustains them, addicts of invisibility: illusionists and simulators.

The butterfly turned into a leaf, the man turned into a woman, but also anamorphosis and trompe-l'oeil, do not copy, do not define and justify themselves on the basis of true proportions; rather—using the position of the observer, including him in their imposture—they produce the model's verisimilitude, they incorporate its appearance as in an act of pillage, they simulate the model.

The speakers in Plato's dialogues, however, trapped in compulsive classification, worried by the power they produce by dividing in hopes of reducing, manage to dismiss or suppress—and thus inaugurate an attitude still prevalent in Western thought—the fundamental issue: neither the mechanisms of simulation, nor its relations with the Sophist's logic, but its generative center: who simulates? from where? why? What drive impels the Sophist to mimicry, what compulsion for disguise, for looking like someone else, for representation, for gaining access to the world of visible proportions by disturbing the model's proportions so that imitated proportions seem real?

In the West, or in Western technique as outlined in Platonic dialogue, the only answers we find to that question are too immediate, too assertive, too anxious to assure presence. In the East you could say that knowledge is itself a state of body, in other words, a being composed, a simulation of being—of being *that* knowledge—which merely recalls the simulative nature of all being—when manifested as *that* being.

In order to know what simulates, then, it will be necessary to go to the space where knowledge neither occurs as a binary function nor arises in the interstice, the magnetism or antagonism of opposing pairs, but where the calm, prepared body receives rather than conquers it, without pillaging something external.

The reverse of knowledge as a possession—among us Westerners, language and things are also possessed—, in the East, at the heart of its great theogonies—Buddhism, Taoism—we find not a full presence, god, man, logos, but a *generative emptiness whose metaphor and simulation is visible reality*, and which, when truly experienced and understood, becomes liberation.

It is the Void, or the initial zero, which in its mimesis and simulation of form projects a one from which the entire series of numbers and things will begin, the initial explosion not of an atom of hypermatter—as postulated by current cosmological theories—but of pure non-presence that, transvestized in pure energy, engenders the visible world with its simulacrum.[7]

Born from and functions of that nothing which is most present when imitations of the model are most intense, camouflage most successful, analogies and usurpations most precise—this is how the phenomena enumerated here must be read, for, seen from original emptiness, they themselves are no more than the theatricality and maximum saturation of all other phenomena.

II. ANAMORPHOSIS

What you say would have another meaning, or more than one meaning, if in each instance you could know who is speaking to what. This is also true for what you see, once you recognize the woof of the canvas as desire.

François Wahl

The reader of anamorphosis, in other words, the reader who, thanks to his own displacement, discovers a figure beneath the apparent amalgam of random colors, shadows, and lines or the reader who discovers the other, "real" image beneath the explicit, enunciated image is not far from analytic practice because of the oscillation implicit in his effort: "quite the contrary, his therapeutic action must be defined in essence as a double movement thanks to which the *image*, diffuse and broken at the start, is regressively assimilated into the real, in order to be progressively disassimilated from the real, in other words, restored to its own reality."[1] In the precise exercise of a baroque reading of anamorphosis, an initial movement, parallel to that of the analyst, in effect assimilates the "broken and diffuse" image into the real; but a second, strictly baroque gesture of distancing and specifying the object, a critique of the figurative, dissimilates the object from the real: that reduction to its own technical mechanism, to the theatricality of simulation, is the baroque *truth* of anamorphosis.

Frontal reading: a pearly, bone-shaped seashell placed tangentially in the foreground of Holbein's *The Ambassadors*, a disproportionate frontispiece held up by nothing other than its shadow on the marmoreal geometry, on a precise marquetry—that of the mosaic in the chancel of Westminster Abbey—, hangs from an invisible thread. Or it might be a sepia bone, an osseous spaceship, one of Dalí's soft watches—as suggested by Lacan. In any case, the obvious reference to the sea evokes the baroque age of Manuel I: trips, the East, armillary spheres, anchors, and ropes.

Jean de Dinteville, Seigneur of Polisy, and Georges de Selve, Bishop of Lavour, the ambassadors, stand on either side of a piece of furniture where the quadrivium of the liberal arts is displayed: on its upper shelf, a celestial globe, a torquetum (an astronomical instrument whose possession was reserved for "people of importance in this world"), a book, and a sundial; on its lower shelf, a terrestial globe, a carpenter's square, and a pair of compasses, a lute, and two books—*L'Arithmétique des Marchands*, by Petrus Apianus (Ingolstadt, 1527) and *Gesangbüchlein*, by Johann Walter (Wittenberg, 1524), which is open to a chorale by Luther, with some musical scores in rolls, or flutes beside it.

The lute is a formal analogy of the shell, just as the rolls of music or flutes stacked on the lower shelf are a formal analogy of the scepter that Jean de Dinteville holds absentmindedly in his right hand.

The objects and their metonymies or formal analogies outline a cross in the foreground of the painting, similar to the cross printed over the skull on pirate flags or bottles of poison.

Marginal reading: once the displaced subject—located at the edge of the picture, the design on the canvas (the surface of discourse)—has access to the second meaning, the seashell becomes a skull. *Vanity of representation*: fallacy of images and futility of portraits and emblems—the astronomical and musical still life—, the skull symbolizes the impermanence and ephemeralness of the ambassadors' mission, the death which brings that mission to a close in the illusory nature of all representation. Or if you prefer: there is a flip side to all discourse and it is revealed only by the timely displacement of the listener who, apparently outside of or indifferent to its enunciation, redistributes its figures—the rhetorical figures of discourse, the emblematic figures of the image. The supposedly careless and random organization of manifest discourse, the formal constellation created without apparent motive as that discourse is heard or viewed (the metonymic cross of *The Ambassadors*), the analysand's repetitions, mistakes, infatuations, omissions, and silences will tell the reader in which direction to shift his position, the object of which fantasm he should replace, with which position of the subject in the fantasm he should conclude.

Baroque reading: neither seashell nor skull—a meditation with no support—; all that counts is the energy of conversion and the cleverness necessary to decipher the flip side—the other of representation—, the *drive behind simulacrum* which, in *The Ambassadors*, is unmasked emblematically and resolved in death.

"But in his own reaction to the listener's rebuff, the subject will betray, expose to view the *image* that replaces him: In his entreaties, his curses, his insinuations, provocations, and traps, in the fluctuations of his intention with respect to his analyst and which are registered by the analyst, who is immobile but not impassive, the subject *communicates the outline of that image*. Nevertheless, as the subject's intentions become more explicit in his discourse, they are increasingly intermixed with evidence that he presents to flesh them out, fill them with life: he gives form to the cause of his suffering, which he wants here to overcome; here he confides the secret of his failures and the success of his objectives, here he judges his character and his relations with others. In this way, the subject informs the analyst about his behavior as a whole and the analyst, who witnesses that behavior for an instant, finds in it a basis for his critique. After the critique, the subject's behavior reveals to the analyst that the very *image* he has just seen arise is permanently active in that behavior. But the analyst's discovery does not end here, for as the request turns into a plea, the evidence is expanded with appeals to the witness; this involves simple tales that seem to be "extraneous" and which the subject now throws into the flow of his discourse, the random events and fragments of memory that make up his story, with some of the most disconnected cropping up from his childhood. But it is precisely among those fragments that the analyst rediscovers the exact *image* that in his play he has elicited from the subject and whose mark he has seen stamped on his person, that image which he knew very well had a human essence since it provoked passion, since it exercised oppression, but which, just as he himself does with the subject, *was hiding its features from his gaze*."[2]

Anamorphosis and the discourse of the analysand as a kind of hiding: something, which will only be revealed to the subject if he shifts his position, is hidden from him—hence his discomfort. The subject is implicated in the reading of the spectacle, the deciphering of discourse, precisely because the thing he is not at first able to hear or see concerns him directly in his capacity as subject.

What is disquieting here is that the frontal relationship between subject and spectacle cannot be considered something acquired with the certainty of a premise.

If, since Alberti, perspective has been presented as a rationalization of the gaze, as the "costruzione legittima" of its hierarchical organization of figures in space and the objective reality of their operation, anamorphosis—"secret perspective" (Dürer), the marginal and perverse operation of that legitimacy—has been associated since its invention with the occult sciences, with hermeticism, and magic (Niceron).

Since its beginnings, perspective has worked like a clock, or like the smooth-running, well-greased mechanism of the age, like hydraulic machines, and automata (Salomon de Caus): immediately legible, nonfigurative poetry, clear efficient reconstruction. Anamorphosis, on the other hand, first gives the impression of opaqueness, and, through the displacement it implies for the subject, reconstructs the mental process of allegory, which is grasped when thought abandons direct, frontal perspective in order to position itself obliquely in relation to the text, as Galileo already maintained.

Furthermore: the obscurity of forms contained within other forms, of disguise,[3] false measurement and distorted truth following from camouflage or transvestism, is related to the occult to such an extent that it becomes identified with evil: "It seems to me that those [anamorphosic] paintings were done in order to depict visions of gloomy dreams or witches' sabbaths, and they are capable of producing only sadness or terror and even of causing the fetuses of pregnant women to be aborted or deformed. I do not believe they can be used to represent natural, pleasing themes."[4]

Through symptoms, the body can accidentally assume—by falling, for example, or losing one's balance—what a subject needs without realizing it—in this case: "there is no one to support me"—: symptoms are the tattooed conversion of things unsaid, the mark of things unbearable to hear. Through anamorphosis, painting can reveal (with disquieting closeness, by masking it in a misleading form, hung above the floor, in the foreground) the ultimate image, the image that is only perceived when the departing subject—*le sujet que se barre*—, who is about to leave the room where he came upon this representation, who is disappointed and has given up hope of understanding the hieroglyphic in nacre, looks, as if to bid farewell, to the left, looks *sinistrally*, and, as in an analytic rebus, at that instant he sees her, the Sinister One, in the macabre splendor of her osseous coat of arms, raging before the terrestrial measurements—Perspective and Music—and the celestial ones—Astronomy: laughing in the foreground, the Mother-of-Bone advances and splits the viewer's final glance.

Opaqueness, the indecipherable in the foreground. Andy Warhol will end the age of legibility in painting, and for this reason the opaque will no longer be stated. By moving aggressively accessory elements to the plane of the picture's exclusive subject, Warhol even eliminates the very notion of plane, along with any conceptual residues of perspective implicit in that notion.

Holbein/Warhol: the provocation of analytic activity through excess opaqueness, through the announcement of supplementary codification when the illegible constitutes the foreground of the picture, or through excess transparency, a fury of realism, the cipher of a theatricality opposed to all interpretation. In Pop it's all the same, all the same to all:[5] a single plane, with neither hierarchies nor halogenous referents—not even "life," indistinguishable in this gesture from the work; death, rather, inscribed in the mechanized drive of repetition.

It is true that Magritte offers the same legibility, the immediacy of a capture, the brutal and instant grasping of the "theme," but in him there is a *simulation of transparency* present only in relation to an underlying density, which, because of its hermeticism, can only become figurative beneath the luminous evidence of certain emblems or beneath the representations of fantasy, which is suspect because of its excessive graphicness. Such laws and procedures would derive from heraldry, never from stylistics.

Warhol and the hyperrealists state objects with excessive clarity, until they get those objects seesawing once again on their oneiric or hallucinated flip sides. In Warhol this takes the form of a repetition that uses the subject as a witness to the essential monotony of everything the artist finds interesting, as if the law of return were his most secret clue. For this reason, the only companion to that violence of clarity is an identical *indifference*; a calm apotheosis, free from technical arrogance—in Pop—or conceptual anchorage, which with equal *detachment* takes posssession of whatever, whether person or thing, falls into its hands, of the copy, or, caught up in the drive of repetition, of the copy of the copy, until it blurs or wears out—the whole museum must be filled with a single image.

Neither a subversion of the image by pointing not so much to it as to the systems that codify it, nor a metaphysics of the figurable. The only wonder is from programmed boredom, the repeatable, recalcitrant aversion to all discourse not part of its own tautology, to all analysis that is not somewhat swept up, swallowed, included—like the clichés that constitute the paintings—in the oppression of its own repetition. Analytic listening: don't start from an enigma or an explicit question, as in anamorphosis, but—Warhol and Estes—from an open, almost flashy rejection, from an obviousness and simplicity of impression—in the typographical sense of that term. From a defiant, banal appearance.

From the point of view of a pragmatic theory of communication, anamorphosis would be the best definition of a reality *created* by information: "And the most dangerous delusion of all is that there is only one reality. What there are, in fact, are many different versions of reality, some of which are contradictory, but all of which are the results of communication and reflection of eternal, objective truths."[6]

Among the concepts with which a pragmatic theory of communication operates, anamorphosis corresponds totally to that of *disinformation*: "knots, impasses and delusions as may come about in the *voluntary* process of actively seeking or of *deliberately dissimulating* information."[7] In Holbein's *Ambassadors*, the legible apparition of the skull, which implies the vanishing not only of enigmatic form, but also that of characters and of stratified still life, could be compared disinformationally to the reverse return, in war, of a code transmitted by the enemy—treacherously devised by him in order to mislead, to get operations running backwards, to slow down or confuse—and to the code's reconstruction, thanks to the key provided in the form of a real message by a double agent, or to its collapse in a farce of detail, an absurd threat.

In 1943 the allies[8] suspected that German military intelligence was running a spy ring out of Lisbon, composed of at least three members—Ostro I, II, and III, two of whom operated in Great Britain, the other in the U.S.A. A notorious British agent, who later defected to the Soviet Union, set out for Lisbon to investigate the cunning of the Ostros and their clever spymaster, a certain Fidrmuc. After working arduously to decipher their messages, the agent discovered on the one hand that the Ostros were no more than heteronomous elements of the ubiquitous Fidrmuc, and, on the other hand, that in order to make his espionage more credible, the efficient informer relied solely on persistent rumors, newspaper clippings, and his "fertile imagination." The ring and Fidrmuc's multiple personality were destroyed with the same efficiency that their inventor had used to fabricate them: messages whose truth could be easily verified, but which contradicted those from the Portuguese "group" were sent to the Germans. One further point of clarification (and baroque detail): according to the annals of espionage, Fidrmuc was an esthete: he asked to be paid in art objects, which, it is true, he resold. I will not rule out the possibility that he had read Pessoa.

The transposition of forms and the metaphor of the subject—in the literal sense as well: displacement of the spectator—implied by anamorphosis do not in one sense contradict another use of that term: "name given to a group of changes observed in certain lichens and other cryptogams" (Littré's *Diccionaire*). In an imaginary botany—in other words, a more generalized one—it can be argued that tuberoses devise sophisticated anamorphoses. Provided, that is, the male bumblebee gets the show "erected," when instead of the receptive, tempting belly of the female, he discovers that he has been confused by the similarity of forms and has penetrated the petals on the corolla of an orchid, the ophrys, which are minutely arranged in the form of a sexual organ. An olfactory anamorphosis—the plant emits volatile compounds among which have been identified chemical bodies contained in the sexual secretions that attract the male bumblebee—and a utilitarian anamorphosis—as it penetrates the simulated sex, the insect is smeared with pollen, which, tricked once again, it will carry to another flower, thus effecting reproduction.[9]

In conclusion: although it employs two authentic Greek roots, the word *anamorphosis* starts from a fictitious etymology: from a simulation.

III. TROMPE L'OEIL

Had one of my images, cast into the world, taken my place and relegated me to the role of reflected image? Had I summoned the Prince of Darkness and was he appearing to me in my own likeness?

> Italo Calvino, "In una rete de linee que s'intersecano," *Se una noite d'inverno un viaggiatore,* Einaudi, 1979

Sensory failure: sight falters; touch must intervene to verify, and refute, what the gaze—victim of sights's naïveté or the precise arrangement of some artifice—assumes to be true: simulated depth, feigned space, apparent perspective, or the excessive—and therefore suspect—compactness of objects, the insistent clarity of their contours, the arrogance of their textures.[1]

At one stroke, fingers quash falsification: neither bright corridors, nor gardens, nor decks of cards scattered as if they had been hurled on marble by an angry loser, nor broken glass, flowers, or fruits: nothing but paint, oils on wood, canvas, a tense, saturated surface in possession of a solvent, credible code, of a convincing vocabulary: that of representation.

Such efficacy, that of making visible the nonexistent, does not start, however, from the affirmation and apotheosis of a personality, a style—although it does start from a technique—, but, quite the contrary, from their maximum dissimulation, their cancellation: the more anonymous the execution, the less it exhibits or denounces brushwork, draftsmanship—labor—, the more successful the trompe-l'oeil. The still-life makes explicit its discrepancy with the referent, its distance from the motif, that *décalage* with the real which is the measure of style. Trompe-l'oeil, whose very definition is the ability to pass for the referent, to codify it, leaving out nothing, to the point of total identification, and thus deny "art," technique, only works when there is a denial of any fluctuation on the part of the signifier, which is hidden as such here, with the two laminas adhering to each other as closely as possible, most separated from the signifier and its palpable, real referent when the style is most ostentatious. Trompe-l'oeil thus achieves a quietude and an apparent forgetfulness of the activity identified as the mark of the subject; this is a "privative state" of the subject and his "personality," that very much resembles a silence: the *stasis* of representation's chatter.

Dissimilar objects in a certain disorder that bespeaks recent use neither aspire to the signature, the stamp of the artist, to the category of esthetic entities, nor assert their residence on the canvas; but, quite the contrary, they inhabit the space of man's gestures, as if to shy away from all frames, all metaphysics—exiles in the oblivion and the wear and tear of everyday life.

"That universe of fabrication obviously excludes terror, just as it excludes all style. The concern of the Dutch painters is not to rid the object of its qualities in order to free its essence but, quite the opposite, to accumulate the secondary vibrations of its appearance, since it is not forms or ideas but layers of air, surfaces, that must be incorporated into human space. The only logical solution in this type of painting is to coat matter with a kind of *glacis* on which man can move without damaging the object's use-value."[2]

Trompe-l'oeil, which was invented precisely to simulate thickness, immediate, credible presence, depth, seems—because of that same insistence on being-there—to summon our gaze, as if attempting to capture it, make it glide over smooth, polished planes, over objects shiny with use, or, on the other hand, by inverting that summons, seems to turn its own *platitude* into a gaze, to watch us in order to provoke dimension, in order to hollow out its single plane, since "depth occurs only at the moment the spectacle itself slowly turns its shadow toward man and begins to look at him."[3]

But the glance directed at us by trompe-l'oeil, its view of us, has a specificity or limit: it arises as if from a center, a vanishing point, or from the virtual hollow of a scale model. Never tangential or displaced, as in anamorphosis, it is always coherent and compact: a laser.[4] This is because those objects, which gaze at us in order to establish depth, can only do so from within the reassuring and reliable interior of the frame: unlike the still life, where objects can be cut off or broken by that frame, in trompe-l'oeil, the whole process is jeopardized if such a break occurs, and this requirement is as fundamental as the anonymity of the brush stroke or the verisimilitude of size. The genre does not admit of the least disproportion, the least emphasis from enlargement, the inevitable grandiloquence of any expansion. Such realism pervades it as a condition of its creditability: if there are crumpled papers, old engravings, invoices, official documents, or letters, not only are they authentic and even identifiable, but their appearance on a vertical wooden board proves they have required the appropriate tacks, strings, or tapes, which are excessively "cited" or visible; sequins, combs, penknives, scissors, and even feathers assume their true proportions and even their weights, as in an intransigent *profession of realism* that admits no variations, innovations, or disagreements. What is more, the objects of trompe-l'oeil must not be moved because of the fixed rules that govern their effects: it takes only a new source of light, a different height or a change in their mounting for shadows and dimensions to *confess* the trick and for the materiality of things, the depth of perspective, the fictitious breach of chandeliers and windows to be reduced to a tedious exercise, an academic diversion, the frustrated effort of an imposter.

In some of Andy Warhol's films, the diegesis, the time of the story, the duration of the fiction, corresponds to the spectator's real time: if a man sleeps, his sleep lasts eight hours. The film time admits neither ellipsis nor contraction; in concert with the time that flows outside the screen, it runs parallel to that in the movie theater and—this coincidence is the "theme" of the film—is indistinguishable from it.

Trompe-l'oeil postulates this analogy, this identity, but in relation to space: in order for the illusion to take shape, the air around the objects must be our own, the shadows they cast must be proportionate and similar to those of the spectator's body, the relations between them must be consistent with the relations they will establish with him, as if the intention of the genre were precisely to forget that from which there can be no escape and without whose limits the genre itself would be nullified: the frame.

In trompe-l'oeil, then, everything—silence, frontal viewing, unity of space—summons equilibrium, stability, or repose. This formal *homeostasis*, however, is seen to be constantly opposed, refuted by its motif, by what is represented, as if the *serenity of the signifier* were no more than the container, the wrapping of contradictory, unstable forces, of antipodal energies that disturb objects and cause them to seesaw back and forth—imbalances and falls avoided an instant before they occur. Or perhaps movement is arrested at its point of maximum concentration, when the gesture reaches its zenith and its definition: emerging from chiaroscuro and beside a table whose cloths receive and reflect the faint light of late afternoon, above showy plates of fruits and oysters, the drinker raises his cup as if to offer the master painter a chance to display his technique by catching the transparency of white wine; emphatic and convivial, he "thrusts" his hand from the painting—the grammatical denotation of the trompe-l'oeil is the quotation mark—eloquent and *bambochard*, he looks at us and "extends" his hand: trompe-l'oeil is realized in that toast, in the epiphany of that gesture.

In trompe-l'oeil, in that snapshot avant la lettre, everything breaks apart and tumbles: the glass panes in the door of a cupboard containing notes and letters have just been smashed, as if the untimely blow of a stone had preceded the painter's gaze;[5] on the table, in another painting, a cup has just fallen over. If there are curtains, they are half-drawn; if doors, they are half-open; if documents, they are yellowed and jumbled; if there are birds, they have just been caught, they are still bloody, and their eyes are frightened and glassy, their feathers iridescent. One of the fruits has just been bitten into or recently peeled—a golden spiral:

orange rind—; *putti* slip on clouds; the door of a cage has been carelessly left open; servants peer through keyholes; dwarves in red jackets pull furiously on the chains of a monkey set on a Corinthian capital or stumble as they ascend the stairway that leads them to the mythological banquet or the heroic feast; if a cat appears, it is sure to be looking at us merrily, or scrutinizing with great interest the gestures of a Benedictine monk in his cell, or getting ready to pounce mercilessly on a rat.

The definition of trompe-l'oeil as a pure Circensian simulation of reality, as a deceptive but verisimilar dubbing of the visible, meets with such skill in the sculptors of American hyperrealism that sometimes the model can pass for an ineffective although detailed reconstruction of the "original" that is the copy: the work.

An American matron, in painted wax, rests for a moment, leaning against the wall as if she were overcome by an indisposition that shows clearly in her bewildered gaze and her perspiration, or as if she were terrified by her own acquisitive excess, which the bag of groceries, stuffed to bursting and pressed against her chest, and the supermarket cart—a Pop cornucopia—exposes as an uncontrollable drive.

On old newspapers—blots of ink spread open on the sidewalk—protected by the dense foul-smelling heat that rises through the subway grate, three drunken bums doze on the Bowery in the early morning in the quiet of the urban winter, dream perhaps, since their mouths are half-open and slobbery, talk in their sleep—in a language that is not English—wet themselves in their much-mended, heavy greyish clothes, in the jackets with grimy sleeves that are too big for them, talk to themselves some more, clutching yesterday's sour, empty bottles like shipwrecked sailors.

Having just separated, they are still panting, not looking each other in the eye, his sex is wet, already limp, smeared, dripping with semen: a slender whitish thread suspended from his member, a precise, almost straight line that runs from the woman's heaving belly near her pubis, down her hips, to the floor of the gallery and from there climbs up the boy's hips, becomes thinner, hyaline, on his skin, like a brush stroke of varnish, until it reaches his sex. Now that their obscene whispers are silenced, only that trail joins them. They part slowly. They are uncoupled, unglued: they will turn away from each other, each to his own space: glutted and rival animals, voracious and sated.

Duplication of reality in the image, the occasional achievement of a hypertrophic degree of precision, a scrupulous simulation, an extravagance of detail: to this perversion the practitioner of trompe-l'oeil sees his efforts limited, like an envious and maniacal demigod. Not so the fan of such impostures: by combining trompe-l'oeil with its model, or, rather by confronting the object and its simulacrum on a single plane of reality, like two versions of the same entity, he can create something of a trompe-l'oeil squared, a larger pleasure in the arrangement of imitations, another enjoyment of that endless game of the double in which none of the versions holds claim to precedence or substance, in which there is no hierarchy of verisimilitude, in other words, no ontological priority.

Bernard Palissy enlivened the stock patterns of sixteenth-century ceramics with crabs and asparagus in relief; he also revolted refined classical diners with snakes and lizards crawling on serving bowls, coiled into spouts and handles; posterity paid dubious tribute to his cleverness: for two centuries the most prolific factories in Europe reproduced ad nauseum every known fruit and vegetable, from the most humble to those whose origins awarded them in those days the distinction of inaccessibility. Tables were filled with artificial olives, eggplants, nuts, rather simplified pineapples, almonds, radishes that brightened cautious still lifes with a touch of bright red, various kinds of melons, and even with an overabundance of hard-boiled eggs.

A customary practical joke of the period, but one whose humor wore thin with the apocryphal proliferation of lesser fruits, consisted of presenting wedding banquets and even Sunday dinners by setting manufactured fruits and ceramic vegetables among real fruits and vegetables, which in comparison to their shiny copies were less appetizing—pallid country greens from the backyard.[6]

A few centuries later, assisted by photography's natural although mechanical trompe-l'oeil, an artist was to reproduce the confrontation occasioned by Bernard Palissy's ceramics. Bernard Faucon begins with familiar surroundings: the rather rundown, untidy room of a French country house, an iron bed with enormous feet, faded prints on the walls, scapulars, pictures of saints hanging askew, a faulty electrical outlet, peeling walls, cobwebs, and dust. Or perhaps we see a more inviting breakfast: the floor is tiled, the tablecloth, although torn, is embroidered: bread and *gaufrettes* on the table; on the wall in the background, an indecipherable allegory hangs in a showy, ornate frame, also a photomontage, and, next to it, the image of a child encircled by a wreath, as if to suggest a gymnastic trophy or a funeral commemoration.

In this setting, which is simultaneously neutral and morbid, Bernard Faucon places the objects of his mad collection: mannequins of children in the most familiar and natural of positions compose scenes, dialogues, small family gatherings or entertainments, "sets" from a provincial shopwindow or from the attic of some nostalgic turn-of-the-century antiquarian.

Mingled with these pearly pink mannequins in their mischief and games are some real children who are dressed like them and carefully made-up in the waxy tones of mannequins or death masks. The group is motionless, fixed, embalmed by the photograph: Pompeian dogs petrified as they leap, scarabs in paperweights.

Yet a further example: Pierre Moliner, dressed like a woman, posing with one of his evil dolls—his death revealed the morbid, lethal nature of this game—, vampires made up like participants in a sadistic or cheap ritual, in officially pornographic poses, purposely stereotyped and grotesque: the artist modeled them after his own image as a transvestite, imitating his female-double, that woman whose image he used to *correct*, modify, criticize not only his real body but even his own identification pictures, which he made up so they would resemble that transvestite.

Martin Battersby notes the exercise in alterity realized by photographer and model Patrick Litchfield as he portrays himself making a routine gesture: with a lighter, he quite casually lights the cigarette held between the lips of a dreamy young man in a nondescript set. The smoker is Litchfield's exact replica in fiberglass. In the background, but equally present and clear, two other passersby are about to meet and start up a conversation, or perhaps they cross paths indifferently without recognizing each other—they both seem to be concentrating on where they are going, to be watching some external and invisible signal: these passersby are also reproductions of their author. Only a few discrepancies in their clothing personalize, bestow a margin of fictitious identity on the four versions of Patrick Litchfield, reduced by his own technique to a mere number in a limitless numeration.

The coincidence between copy and model, between characters and wax, or fiberglass and flesh and blood, does not always draw attention to the artifice of duplication and thus favor the live element of the couple; it also happens quite often that, on the contrary, what "acts," what is endowed with energy in that pair of identical forms and opposite substances, is not the man but his *simili*, even if that energy is made explicit only in the simulation of a glance. Painting has created a precedent:

From the ceiling in the bridal chamber of the Palazzo Ducale in Mantua, some personages of the court, from Moors to angels, look at us looking at the frescos that illustrate the robustness and lineage of the Gonzaga family; one of them, a *putto* or angel who is holding his own crown, has landed dangerously outside the balustrade over which the courtiers are peering, as if to suggest a game of levitation or perhaps to materialize the gaze of the elevated spectators an instant before it rests on us and encloses us in its enveloping, alien cone. That scrutiny from above, centered although plural, conditions and provokes our own; we cannot enter without being viewed, without being *reviewed* beforehand, nor confront the authoritarian although amiable face of the leader without the tacit consent of his followers. While they spy on our movements as we face the picture and their gaze follows the breaks, intensity, and shifts of ours, we can look first at the cohesive, tight-knit group that, like an emblematic color, consolidates the flow of a bloodline. Then we can pause at the docile groom who approaches through the trees, leading a compact, classic white horse, at the legs of the pages, the relief of the fabrics, at the canopy, the capitals, until we come to the nosy, sarcastic face of the dwarf, the only character in the fresco who looks at us directly. She seems inquisitive and annoyed, though, as if she wanted to exclude us from the family's private life or send us out of the room, and her mockery brings Mantegna's cycle of the gaze to its conclusion.

In 1784, in the Orangery Theater in Warsaw, Jan Bogumil Plersch continued this relationship and developed it far more radically, incorporating it into his Borges-like design when he conceived and painted trompe-l'oeil characters who, always watching the same imaginary drama, nevertheless blended in with the real audience. Since Plersch worked from living models, his painted figures could scrutinize their doubles as they arrived for the nightly performance, so long as fashions did not drastically change and provided that those doubles, in order to exchange a glance with their portraits, turned toward a nonexistent corridor that was every bit as lifelike as the motionless spectators. A legend attributes the same cleverness to Paolo Veronese.

The balance or feigned equilibrium between the model and his double, between man and mannequin, seesaws visibly in the theater of Tadeusz Kantor,[7] and in an unpredictable way. Seated at their desks, busy and well-behaved as if they were playing school, a few old people are seen on stage. Silence. One of them, almost inadvertently, in an outburst of heroism, dares to destroy the *still photo*: he lifts a finger. Another turns toward him, and slowly, compulsively, imitates him. Soon the class has regained its uniformity through the rebellious gesture, which repetition has rendered harmless. The death instinct has taken shape in the *minimal* interstice of repetition.

Alongside the actors, some seated mannequins. Wax children that resemble them too closely. Kantor is also present, but not to direct the actors. A marionette directs them. The puppet positions them and leads them into orthogonal, mechanical movements of hinges and creaking joints, into perpetual repetition, or, rather, into silence, fixity, and death, which "has seized the characters like a stranglehold, reducing them to a single gesture, to utensils, hairdresser's heads for displaying coiffures, stumps of arms and legs, according to Schulz's principle."

"The actor must be created, right there, before our very eyes, but at an infinite distance; it is necessary to renew continually the crucial moment when *someone appears*, someone almost identical to oneself, the self with a dead man's face; *only that oscillation between likeness and likeness defines the actor*.

"But how would the actor dare something so bold? How was he going to find his pose if he did not have the marionette as a model? *An almost ludicrous proposition: a marionette on stage directs the actor.* By the way it sits beside the physical man—and yet remains separate from him across the whole distance of the inert—, a marionette teaches the man how he should present himself to the audience: from mimicry to schism."

Kantor: *"In my theater a mannequin must turn into a MODEL that embodies and conveys a profound sentiment of death and the condition of the dead: a model for the LIVING ACTOR."*

The end—for now—of this progression toward simulation that began with the initial duplication represented by trompe-l'oeil, of this *escalade* toward the *copy's vengeance on the model*: the inscription, on the living, of the inert.

Gilbert and George mount self-exhibits in museums and galleries. Crossed arms, eyeglasses of an accountant or notary, tweed suits, white collars and ties, immobility and silence—it could be, perhaps, an empty moment in a Beckett conversation, when a "suspension" of the content confronts the characters with their artificial, gratuitous, unbearably nonessential nature: the banality of their pose, conventionality of their dress, stereotypicalness of their situation.

Clearly, then, in its saturation of the inanimate, its return of the inert double, the performance by Gilbert and George surpasses Kantor's teaching mannequin, which appears on stage, supervises. Gilbert and George have abolished the model—the one that would be their wax replica—they have excluded it from the performance, as if to *in-corporate it*, to internalize it physically, turning it into nature, an *almost insignificant* death, denounced, nevertheless, by the rigidity of their gestures, the pallor of their faces sickened by neon, the coarse efficacy of their bodies, less suitable for life than for modeling the English cut of their clothing.

It seemed to me that an approach to simulation might comprise the three instances I have noted: copy, anamorphosis, and trompe-l'oeil. In conclusion, I believe that those three instances correspond to the Imaginary—the drive of simulation by virtue of which, in order to be, one must become a figure, and the figure is always other—; the Symbolic—anamorphosis can only be conceived within the framework of a code of representation, more particularly that of perspective, and at the site where the subject is brought into the picture—; and the Real—since trompe-l'oeil, beyond the step from eye to hand, testifies to the *surplus* found in the presentation of any presence.

Perhaps it was not by chance that my point of departure was universal illusion, was reality as an emphatic "bluff" of the nothing, as suggested by Buddhism, and that I conclude with the domination of the living by the inanimate and by repetition. Beyond the pleasure of what it stages, like predictable, familiar fiestas, simulation enunciates the void and death.

PAINTED ON A BODY

TOWARD A HYPERTELIC ART

I. Color Sutures

At the time of the equinoctial tides, certain ciliate creatures retreat too far across the sand, flee too far inland. When the sea calms down, they are unable to reach it again: they die in exile, trying to return to the increasingly distant water, to travel in reverse the path that an irresistible impulse, inscribed in them since birth, forced them to follow by imbuing them with its energy.

Those animals—or the genetic knowledge that runs through them, their harmony with the gravitational forces that control the tides—pay for their excess with their lives. Hypertelic creatures: they have pressed beyond their goals, as if from the very beginning, and to a disproportionate degree, encoded in their nature they had a lethal impulse for supplement, simulacrum, and pageantry—since the same futile display can be found in the mimetic ornamentation developed by various species of butterflies.[1]

Holger Holgerson's body paintings on Veruschka, his "Mimicry-Dress-Art," are located in that space traveled in excess, in a knowledge that moves beyond its object to the point of provoking the object's disappearance: hypertelic art.

When the brush is applied to the canvas—as in another context we apply the gaze: the matter with which we anoint the real—, color performs its work of illusion. Constructing a disappearance like the one seen through an open window—the window or pyramid of perspective—, drawing establishes a vanishing point that convention has located in infinity, but whose position is rigidly codified on the surface of the canvas. There is a maximum degree of separation, or difference between the support—the canvas, the representation's stretcher—, and the illusion staged on it.

In contrast, in Veruschka's "camouflages"—I will insist on that defensive, warlike metaphor—, the separation between support—body/canvas, body/page—and representation—a dress painted on a body—has been reduced to zero, making the coincidence total: there is no interstice, no void to "distance" the *phantasmal adherence* between stretcher and illusion.

Color sutures, weaves into the real the precise and apparently fixed superposition of those dresses *plus vrai que nature* "on" a body that can scarcely signify as such.

But "dress-art" goes much further. Not at the limit, but beyond all limits, it is a question of erasing, abolishing, assuring the disappearance of the body/support through total identification with the surface that backs it, with the ground where it lights, becomes fixed. Camouflage: not to seem the aggressor. Not to have to defend oneself. To counteract the enemy's scrutinizing, voracious eye by resorting to an apotropaic death: theater of invisibility.

Veruschka and Holgerson—her body is a miniature he draws minutely—fascinated by fashion—which is a form of death—and tattooing, have practiced "dress-art" for many years. In an early series of photographs, Veruschka "wore" striped, spangled, art deco dresses that were torn, formal, or frivolous.

But the simulacrum of fashion, the daily application—in both senses of the word—of her dress were not enough. Like the butterfly, giving in to a hypertelic impulse and threatened by no enemy, from the sheer desire for metamorphosis, for useless expenditure and ornamentation, turns into a leaf—and even further, the height of cleverness, into a sick leaf—, into bark, bud, or moss, Veruschka, suddenly a man, a man who turns into a woman or is mesmerized by the image of a woman, pressed beyond her goals. Woman-wall. The angle of a window, a damp old wooden door, split, robbed of its nails, forgotten in the corner of a German farm. A pipe. Nothing. A stain on a wall. An electric switch. Total identification with background. Little by little her body disappears, becomes a texture identical to that of the plane that backs it, devoid of volume, edges, bound by a single law: extravagance; it is attracted, magnetized by the invisible, by what is apparent.

All that matters are the lines of color, the disappearance of contours—which is achieved by imitating, directly on the "subject," the surface of the ground: the excessive knowledge of suturing.

II. Fetish

In the exhibiton of the fetish there is a frigid theatricality, an excessively calculated staging that, because it is modeled on ostentation, belongs to *caravaggismo*: light projected harshly—a concise method for trapping the gaze—is concentrated on one part of the body, or on one of its metonymies: the face; a hand in the act of striking; a turban; calloused, porous feet; rags. Such sectarian illumination relegates the remainder of the body—a paradoxical remainder—to an anonymous, distant zone excluded from representation and desire: unworthy of erection, shadowy and awkward.

Torturing and tattooing belong to the same list of dismemberments through factitious fragmentation.[2] One part of the body is defined with pain or ink, and by dint of "work," that part is separated from the image of the body as a whole. This decorated or tortured member, marked by its singularity, recalls another: the maternal and phallic one from which all the rest of the body—turned into an unfeeling object, a no-body—has been expelled, exiled.

Only the fragment covered with tattoos—initials, anchors, and hearts always seem to be inscribed, as if by chance, on biceps, the most *erectile* muscles—minutely highlighted with fine ink, or submitted to twisting, to pain, has created the possibility of hardening, of blatant erection, of hitting with its tension.[3] The rest of the body merits only shame: flabbiness and boredom.

"Mimicry-Dress-Art" inverts that fragmentation. In it—in the immediacy of the photographic present, in the *here* that is Veruschka's body painted and worn with the real-life quality of all photos—the entire body is in a state of erection, subjected to absolute visibility or, on the contrary, plunged into a night of ink, devoured by the surface that backs it. The body is like a shield. Spanned by a precise genealogy, a heraldry: a phallic emblem. Or, if you prefer: the entire body is a partial object. But the fetish is fascinating when exhibited because it always appears as the ghost of the separable, of something that can be ripped off: Veruschka's dresses can bleed.

In the Japanese film *Kwaidan* a web of mantras is written on the skin of a monk in order to save him from the nightly summons of evil spirits. But in their haste, the calligraphers, who work their way up from the feet as they cover his coveted body inch by inch, forget an ear. The demons stand over him and pull on that ear until they rip off the piece of unwritten skin.

Everything that is not textual is castratable.

(I fainted in the theater.)

III. Fixity

Fixity belongs to *offensive* mimicry. The intimidating display of eyes, the flashy swelling, the proliferation of scales or spines that transforms the frightened animal into the mask or double of another animal worthier of fear—all this simulacrum becomes fixed exactly as displayed. The same is true of mimicry's other register, the "fake," the falsification of illness. Chewed-up, leprous leaves; excrement: passive simulation of death.

This is because fixity comprises all threats, contains the potential for every possible aggression; no movement, no repulsive or intimidating manoeuvre is better able to dissuade.

Veruschka has chosen photographs because there is something of a *defensive* camouflage in her nonexistent finery: to remove that finery is to rip off her skin. To undress me to make love is to kill me.

Photos fix. They fix their objects in an immobility outside which the entire show of mimicry and get-ups would be consigned to the law of illusion—in motion, of course, these "dresses" would not have the least verisimilitude—, while the entire ceremony of body painting and the exhibition of the painted body would be relegated to the convention of *art*. This exhibition, like all sadistic scenes, can only crystalize its play by presenting it as a *tableau vivant*.[4]

Photos fix. But now I am assigning to the verb "fix" the meaning it has in drug jargon ("to take a fix": to inject oneself), which is to say, photos simultaneously immobilize and delude. No art belongs more intimately to the imaginary, to simulation, no art offers a "high" greater than photography. Nevertheless, photography is an art in which everything has really existed, everything has been.

In her photos, Veruschka's whole body looks at us. Not only her eyes.

Her eyes: canvas, tweed, sequin, buttons, stripes.

Also: wall.

IV. Jataka

I'll end with a jataka.[5]

The story is about a trapped gazelle who submits to hypertelic art in order to save itself: it makes the hunter believe it fell into the trap a long time ago and is already dead. The gazelle goes even further: it simulates not only death but also rot, decay. It dampens the ground, pulls up the surrounding grass, and even scatters some excrement to suggest the throes of death. It lies down, sticks out its tongue, sweats, inflates its stomach as if it were full of putrid fermentation. It lies so still that flies light on it, and crows begin to devour it.

The hunter unties it.

With a leap, the gazelle disappears.

And turns into the Buddha.

NOTES

Translator's Introduction

1. *Written on a Body* comprises all the essays in *Escrito sobre un cuerpo* (Buenos Aires, 1969) and the first third of *La simulación* (Caracas, 1982). In the epigraph, which is from Sarduy's brief introduction to *La simulación*, I have replaced the original Spanish title with the English one. I have also added *Literature* to *Painting*, since many of the earlier essays are set in that space.

2. José Lezama Lima, *La expresión americana* (1957; Santiago de Chile: Editorial Universitario, 1969) 9.

3. Sarduy, who was born in Camagüey, Cuba in 1937, has lived in Paris since 1959, when he went there on a government scholarship to study art criticism. He is now a French citizen.

4. Paul Mann, "Translating Zukofsky's Catullus," *Translation Review* 21-22 (1986): 7.

5. Indeed, to have a full reading of the principles elaborated in *Written on a Body*, it is necessary to witness their transposition in Sarduy's fiction, to experience—for example—the reappearance of many different passages in the strikingly different register(s) glimpsed from time to time in the essays. Fortunately, three of Sarduy's novels are available in English, in translations by Suzanne Jill Levine: *De donde son los cantantes* (*From Cuba with a Song*, in *Triple Cross* [New York: Dutton, 1972]); *Cobra* (New York: Dutton, 1975); *Maitreya* (Hanover, NH: Ediciones del Norte, 1987). *Para la voz*, a collection of Sarduy's radio plays has been translated by Philip Barnard as *For Voice* (Pittsburgh, PA: Latin American Literary Review Press, 1985). For a good introduction in English to Sarduy and his work see Roberto González Echeverría's prologue to Levine's translation of *Maitreya*. ("Excritura/Travestismo," translated by Alfred MacAdam as "Writing/ Transvestism" in *Review* 9 [Fall 1973]: 31-33, appears here in a new version.)

6. *Choteo*, in a Cuban context, is a singular, complex form of verbal jesting or mocking that deserves to be retained in Spanish. Although examples of this phenomenon occur throughout *Written on a Body*, one of the best examples of how it operates in Sarduy's work is his insertion of "the phantom *siguapas*" (and himself) into a passage in "Dispersion" quoted from Cintio Vitier's *Lo cubano en la poesía*. (My thanks here to Oscar Montero's *Name Game: Writer / Fading Writer in "De donde son los cantantes"* [Chapel Hill: NC Studies in the Romance languages and literatures, 1988] for an explanation of this passage [66].) In English, a good discussion of choteo can be found in Gustavo Pérez Firmat's "Riddles of the Sphincter," *Literature and Liminality: Festive Readings in the Hispanic Tradition* (Durham, NC: Duke UP, 1986) 53-84.

From *Yin* to *Yang*

1. *La Nouvelle Justine*, v. VII.

2. That strip or band is the focal point of the topology that serves as metaphor for Jacques Lacan's structural system. See *Écrits* (Paris: Seuil, 1966).

3. "When the children were finally resting, dead, he would kiss them . . . and the ones that had beautiful heads and limbs he would single out to look at more closely, ordering their bodies to be opened cruelly and reveling in the sight of their inner organs. . . . And frequently, . . . accompanied by two men named Corrillaut and Henriet, he sat on the children's stomachs as they died and *laughed* from such great pleasure. . . ." See Procès de Gilles de Rais, documents preceded by an introduction by Georges Bataille (Club Français du Livre, 1959).

4. At the beginning of the seventeenth century, Countess Erzsébet Báthory assassinated 650 girls in her castle, in the name of "her right as a high-ranking noblewoman." See Valentine Penrose, *Erzsébet Báthory, la comtesse sanglante* (Mercure de France, 1965), trans. by Alexander Trochhi as *The Bloody Countess* (London: Calder and Boyars, 1970) and the excellent essay by Alejandra Pizarnik, which concludes: " . . . the countess Báthory reached, beyond all limits, the absolute depths of depravity. This is yet another proof that for human beings absolute freedom is horrible" ("La libertad absoluta y el horror"): *Diálogos* [Mexico], 5, [julio-agosto, 1965]), trans. as "The Bloody Countess" by Alberto Manguel in *Other Fires*, ed. Alberto Manguel [New York: Clarkson N. Potter, 1986] and by Suzanne Jill Levine in *Alejandra Pizarnik: A Profile*, ed. Frank Graziano [Durango, CO: Logbridge-Rhodes, 1987]).

Although these two names appear frequently in writings about Sade, I believe it would be opportune to point out that the Marquis's adventure unfolds on a *phantasmagoric* level, on a plane that society is still unable to assimilate, the plane of *writing*. His wantonness is textual. Aside from a few lozenges containing cantharides (which he gave to some prostitutes from Marseilles and which could be procured so easily that they were referred to with the name of a French statesman) and other minor "offenses," he carried over very little into what is considered reality, scarcely *translated* the truth of his phantoms. For this reason his revolution is intolerable, even to this day.

5. To my knowledge, there are no equivalents of this expression in other languages, and at least in Spanish it seems unlikely to me that there are any. Although Spanish has a great wealth of metaphors for referring to the sexual act, there is no hint of a "little death." Of course, our erotic mythology is full of expressions like "to die of pleasure," etc. But nothing, that I know of, links ejaculation and death.

6. Denis Hollier, "La matérialisme dualiste de Georges Bataille," *Tel Quel* 25 (1966).

7. Even though they last only a fraction of a second, a few glimmers of that *ananda* have been identified by Octavio Paz: in childhood; in love, a state of union and participation; in the poem, a magnetic object, a secret place where opposing forces coincide. Introduction to *El arco y la lira* (Mexico, 1956), trans. by Ruth L. C. Sims as *The Bow and the Lyre* (New York: McGraw-Hill, 1973).

8. Thus, on the level of praxis, sadism would be the affirmation of a duel. Sadistic aggression, with its rhetoric of bondage, would be the affirmation of the Other as pure passivity, as absolute *yin*.

9. Max Kaltenmarck, *Lao Tseu et le taoïsme* (Paris, 1965), trans. by Roger Greaves as *Lao Tzu and Taoism* (Stanford, CA: Stanford U Press, 1969).

10. The phantom of aurification has become explicit in our contemporary erotic mythology. Popular novels and the movies have made us aware of it, exploited it. The most literal (purest) aurification is the one that occurs in a scene from Ian Fleming's *Goldfinger* (London, 1959).

A Pearl Gray Cashmere Fetish

1. (Mexico: Siglo XXI, 1967), trans. by Suzanne Jill Levine as *Holy Place*, in *Triple Cross* (New York: E. P. Dutton, 1972).

2. Roland Barthes, "Le visage de Garbo," in *Mythologies* (Paris: Seuil, 1957), trans. by Annette Lavers as "The Face of Garbo," in *Mythologies* (1972; New York: Hill and Wang, 1980). My classification of the "ages" and other quotations refer to this article.

3. Guy Rosolato, "Étude des perversions sexuelles á partir du fétichisme," in *Le désir et la perversion* (Paris: Seuil, 1967). The "conditions" of the fetish enumerated here are taken from this article.

4. Roland Barthes, *Le Système de la Mode* (Paris: Seuil, 1967), trans. by Richard Howard as *The Fashion System* (New York: Hill and Wang, 1983).

5. This is how a critical reading of José Lezama Lima's *Paradiso* should be undertaken, as an all-embracing metaphor of a whole culture and a conversion into literary discourse of the entire lexicon of knowledge.

Writing / Transvestism

1. Jacques Derrida, *L'écriture et la difference*, 1967, trans. by Alan Bass as *Writing and Difference* (Chicago: U Chicago, 1978).

2. Jean-Louis Baudry, "Écriture, fiction, idéologie," Tel Quel 31.

3. Emir Rodríguez Monegal, "El mundo de José Donoso," *Mundo Nuevo* 12. (The Donoso novel referred to in this essay has been published in Mexico by Joaquín Mortiz). (Published in English as *Hell Has No Limits*, trans. Hallie D. Taylor and Suzanne Jill Levine, in *Triple Cross*.)

The (Textual) Adventure of a Collector of (Human) Skins

1. Maurice Roche, *Compact*, *Tel Quel* Collection, Seuil, 1966.

2. Roman Jakobson, *Essais de Linguistique Générale*, Minuit, 1963.

3. Julia Kristeva, "Pour une sémiologie des paragrammes," *Tel Quel* 29 and *Critique* 239.

About Góngora: Squaring Metaphor

1. Dámaso Alonso, *Luis de Góngora. Las soledades* (Madrid: Sociedad de Estudios y Publicaciones, 1956). In order to study Góngora, Alonso modified Saussure's concept of the syntagma and added to it Bally's idea of progression. In these brief notes and in my quotations from Alonso's work, I have tried to incorporate

into Bally's notion some of the contributions made by contemporary Structuralism, Barthes, and Lacan.

2. I believe that a mirror has been used, although the fact that in *Las Meninas* Velázquez is shown painting with his right hand and not his left, as he would have appeared in a mirror, seems to deny it. The supposed mirror at the back of the room, where the king and queen were probably reflected, is no more justifiable: the dimensions of the monarchs as they are seen in that mirror imply a very limited distance between it and them. On this canvas, whose size coincides with that of the ladies in waiting, Velázquez paints those ladies in waiting and nothing else: the painting does not direct us toward another scene that he might have painted.

It is remarkable that something led civilization to place a real mirror in the small room of the Prado museum where for many years *Las Meninas* was displayed, in exactly the place where the other, virtual mirror must have been located.

3. To the tomb of King Philip III.

Cubes

1. Jacques Derrida, "La clôture de la représentation," in *L'écriture et la différence,* trans. by Alan Bass as "The Theater of Cruelty and the Closure of Representation," in *Writing and Difference.*

2. Quoted by Michel Foucault, "Parler," in *Les mots et les choses*, trans. as "Speaking" in *The Order of Things: An Archeology of the Human Sciences.*

Free Texts and Plane Texts

1. Oscar Masotta, *Arte Pop y Semántica* (Buenos Aires: Instituto Torcuato Di Tella, 1965).

2. Basilia Papastamatíu, *El pensamiento común, textos libres* (Buenos Aires: Ediciones Airón, 1956). Trans. by Ronald Christ as "The Shared Thoughts, Free Prose of Basilia Papastamatíu," in *TriQuarterly* 13-14 (Fall/Winter1968); rpt. in *The TriQuarterly Anthology of Contemporary Latin American Literature*, ed. José Donoso and William Henkin (New York: Dutton, 1969).

3. Claude Lévi-Strauss, *La Pensée Sauvage* (Paris: Plon, 1962), trans. as *The Savage Mind* (Chicago: U Chicago, 1966).

4. Nanni Balestrini, *Come si agisce* (Milan: Feltrinelli, 1963) 209-30.

5. Michel Foucault, *Les Mots et les Choses* (Paris: Gallimard, 1966), and Jacques Lacan, *Écrits* (Paris: Editions du Seuil, 1966).

From the Painting of Objects to Objects that Paint

1. W. Kandinsky, "Über die Formfrage," *Der Blaue Reiter* (Munich, 1912), trans. by Henning Falkenstein as "On the Question of Form," *The Blue Reiter Almanac*, ed. Wassily Kandinsky and Franz Marc, New Documentary Edition ed. Klaus Lankheit (New York: Viking, 1974).

2. I have adapted the list of things in this enumeration from Marcel Jean, *Histoire*

de la Peinture Surréaliste (Paris: Seuil, 1959) 251, trans. by Simon Watson Taylor as *The History of Surrealist Painting* (London: Weidenfeld and Nicholson, 1960) 251.

3. Jean 243.

4. A good many people do not share this opinion. Aldo Pellegrini has recently expressed his disagreement to me.

5. Interview with Gene Swenson, *Art News*, November 1963.

6. Duchamp interviewed on American television, 1955.

7. Françoise Choay, *Dada, Néo-Dada, et Rauschenberg*.

8. Jacques Derrida, *De la grammatologie*, trans. by Gayatry Chakravorty Spivak as *Of Grammatology* (Baltimore, MD: Johns Hopkins U, 1974), and "I y II," in *Critique* 223 and 224 (Dec. 1965 and Jan. 1966).

9. Roland Barthes has already discussed a rhetoric of the photographic image in "Rhétorique de l'image," *Communications* [Paris: Seuil] 4 (Nov. 1964), trans. by Richard Howard as "Rhetoric of the Image," in Roland Barthes, *The Responsibility of Forms* (New York: Hill and Wang, 1985). Philippe Sollers has explored Poussin's work using this method of reading: "La lecture de Poussin," *Tel Quel* 5 (1961).

10. I spoke of these problems in "Peintures et Machines," *France Observateur* [Paris] 754 (Oct. 1964).

Copy / Simulacrum

1. Roger Caillois, *Méduse et Cie* (Paris: Gallimard, 1960), 31.

2. Because transvestites, like insects, are *hypertelic*: they press beyond their goals, they take an excess of precautions, which is often fatal. Their supplementary, exaggerated femininity marks them, gives them away.

3. I do not know if I am the first to do this. I hope that after Roger Caillois's exhaustive allegation in *Méduse et Cie* it is no longer necessary to apologize for anthropocentric arguments. Men and insects are jointly responsible for a single system, and it would be absurd to exclude insects from any human system.

4. The most conclusive, carried out between 1885 and 1932 by the United States Biological Survey and published by W. C. McAtee, examined the viscera of 80,000 birds and proves that, taking into account regional proportions, there were as many camouflaged as uncamouflaged victims in the birds' stomachs: McAtee concludes, then, that mimesis is perfectly useless.

5. Plato 235c.

6. Giles Deleuze, *Logique du sens* (Paris: Minuit, 1969) 292ff; *idem* for the two subsequent quotations.

7. One need only begin a philosophical reading—I won't say religious reading: Buddhism is not a religion—of Chinese painting for the void to arise as a generative principle: "Since in Chinese optics, the Void is not, as one might suppose, something vague or nonexistent, but an eminently dynamic and productive ele-

ment. Related to the idea of vital breaths and the principle of alternation between *Yin* and *Yang*, the Void constitutes the place par excellence where transformations are produced, where Fullness might reach its true plenitude. It is the Void that, by introducing discontinuity and reversibility into a given system, allows the component units of that system to overcome rigid opposition and one-way development, and at the same time allows man the possibility of a comprehensive approach to the universe'' (François Cheng, *Vide et plein*, Paris: Seuil, 1979). Also: Lao-Tzu, *Tao-Te-Ching*, Chap. XL: ''The Ten Thousand Creatures are born from 'to have,' but 'to have' is a product of the Void (*wu*),'' and *Chung-tzu* (Chapter about ''Heaven and Earth''): ''In the beginning there is the Void (*wu*); the Void has no name. From the Void is born the One; the One has no shape.''

Anamorphosis

1. Jacques Lacan, *Écrits* (Paris: Seuil, 1966) 85.

2. Lacan 84. Emphasis added.

3. About this idea, and especially about the concept of anamorphosis used here, see Jurgis Baltrušaitis, *Anamorphoses ou magie artificelle des effets merveilleux*) (Paris: Olivier Perrin, 1969), trans. by W. J. Strachan as *Anamorphic Art* (New York: Harry N. Abrams, 1977).

4. Grégorie Huret (1670), quoted by Baltrušaitis.

5. Patrick Mauriès, *Second Manifeste Camp* (Paris: Seuil, 1979).

6. Paul Watzlawick, *How Real Is Real? Communication, Disinformation, Confusion* (New York: Random House, 1976) xl, trans. as *La réalité de la réalité* (Paris: Seuil, 1978) 7.

7. Watzlawick, *How Real* xiv; *La réalité* 9.

8. Watzlawick, *How Real* 121; *La réalité* 121.

9. ''Natural History of Sexuality,'' an exhibition at the Botanical Gardens in Paris, 1977, and Bertrand Visage, *Chercher le monstre* (Paris: Hachette, 1978) 31.

Trompe-l'oeil

1. From sight, as an instability and drop in perception, to touch, and finally, in this sensory failure, to the paradoxical annulment of values—inherent, nevertheless, in Painting—represented by sight, by the retinal: this contradiction is the starting point for ''Koan, about Tapies,'' in *La simulación*.

2. Roland Barthes, ''Le Monde-Object,'' *Essais Critiques* (Paris: Seuil, 1964) 19-28, trans. by Richard Howard as ''The World as Object,'' *Critical Essays* (Evanston, IL: Northwestern U, 1972) 3-12.

3. Barthes 21.

4. Outside of this privileged point of view, perspective disappears or becomes deformed, as in the permanent stage setting of Vicenza's Teatro Olimpico where the greatest sense of depth is experienced in the royal box.

5. Seeing that the great trompe-l'oeil of this century, *The Bride Stripped Bare by Her Bachelors, Even*, simulates a supplementary dimension—the fourth—, it must not be attributed to chance if the definitive "signing" is linked with a quartering, as its exegete Octavio Paz does not fail to suggest. See *Apariencia desnuda* (Mexico: Era, 1973), trans. by Donald Gardner and Rachel Phillips as *Marcel Duchamp: Appearance Stripped Bare* (New York: Seaver-Viking, 1978).

6. I have taken this example, as well as many others in this fragment, from Martin Battersby's book *Trompe l'oeil: The Eye Deceived* (London: Academy Editions, 1974), one of the few that deals exclusively with the subject. In the absence of a future History of Art that would not be limited to a consideration of this mechanism of simulation as just another "gadget," it is also worth glancing at: Marie-Christine Gloton, *Trompe-l'oeil et décor plafonnant dans les églises romaines de l'âge baroque* (Rome: Edizione di storie e letteratura, 1965); Maurice Henri Pirenne, *Optics, Painting and Photography* (Cambridge: Cambridge U Press, 1970); Ingvar Bergström, *Revival of Antique Illusionistic Wall-Painting in Renaissance Art* (Göteborg, Stockholm: Almquist och Wiksell, 1975) and other works.

7. Polish dramatist and painter, who in 1955 founded the theater *Cricot 2* in Cracow, "a rather hybrid company of real actors, occasional actors, and painters-turned-actors who followed their own paths in Cricot." More recently: *The Dead Class* and his *New Treatise about Mannequins*, which reveals Kantor's debt to Bruno Schultz. Information and quotations about Kantor are from Visage, *Chercher le Monstre* 108-18. Emphasis added.

Color Sutures

1. There is a similar example in *José Lezama Lima: Valoraciones múltiples* (La Habana: Casa de las Americas, 1970) 62. Also in Roger Caillois, *Le Mythe et l'Homme* (1938; Paris: Gallimard, 1972) 113. I proposed a reading of transvestism with respect to mimicry in *Guadalimar* 7.

2. *Fetiche* ("Fetish") comes from the Portuguese *fetisse*, which later became *facticio* ("factitious"), but also, in Spanish, *hechizo* ("enchantment").

3. Hardening: "The text would also be something . . . that was erected monumentally and would have to be read as a kind of hardening" (Roland Barthes, "Supplement," *Art Press* 4 (May-June 1937): 9.

4. Sadistic theatricality has been compared to an *ars combinatoria* that falls into place in the *tableau vivant*. See Roland Barthes, *Sade, Fourier, Loyola* (Paris: Seuil, 1971), trans. by Richard Miller as *Sade/Fourier/Loyola* (New York: Hill and Wang, 1976).

5. *Choix de Jakata:* a collection of stories or fables about the Buddha's incarnations, at times in animals, prior to his historical appearance. Translated into French from the Pali by Ginette Terral (Paris: Gallimard, 1958) 12, and into En-

glish by Robert Chalmers, *The Jataka or Stories of the Buddha's Former Births*, 3 vols. (1895; London: Luzac and Co. for the Pali Text Society, 1969) 1: 47-48.

Other Titles from Lumen, Inc.

Under a Mantle of Stars
Manuel Puig
Translated by Ronald Christ
ISBN: 0-930829-00-X

Dialogue in the Void:
Beckett & Giacometti
Matti Megged
ISBN: 0-930829-01-8

Culture and Politics in Nicaragua:
Testimonies of Poets and Writers
Steven White
ISBN: 0-930829-02-6

Sor Juana's Dream
Edited and translated by Luis Harss
ISBN: 0-930829-07-7

For an Architecture of Reality
Michael Benedikt
ISBN: 0-930829-05-0

Reverse Thunder,
A Dramatic Poem
Diane Ackerman
ISBN: 0-930829-09-3

Space in Motion
Juan Goytisolo
Translated by Helen Lane
ISBN: 0-930829-03-4

Borges in/and/on Film
Edgardo Cozarinsky
Translated by Gloria Waldman and
Ronald Christ
ISBN: 0-930829-08-5

ANGST: Cartography
Moji Baratloo & Cliff Balch
ISBN: 0-930829-10-7

SITES
An annual literary/architectural magazine
ISSN: 0747-9409